T0164005

JAH HILLS

UNATHI SLASHA

CL⬥SH

Copyright © 2019 by Unathi Slasha

ISBN: 978-1-944866-43-3

Cover by Matthew Revert

matthewrevertdesign.com

CLASH Books

clashbooks.com

All rights reserved.

No part of this book may be reproduced in any form or by any electronic or mechanical means, including information storage and retrieval systems, without written permission from the author, except for the use of brief quotations in a book review.

To Grandmother:
for the terrifying tales told in my childhood
To Nancy Morkel: for many reasons

CONTENTS

INTRODUCTION: READ CAREFULLY, HANDLE WITH CAUTION

What you're holding right now is a kind of bomb. I'm not sure I want to tell you how to defuse it. But I can tell you where it was made.

Despatch is a township district of Port Elizabeth, one of the major cities in South Africa, in the Eastern Cape Province. The remains of a stegosaurus were found here in 1903. The area was famous for brick making once, and the idea of "dispatch" comes from the bricks that got shipped out. More recently it's been known for violence. How dangerous it is really is a matter of perspective, but it might make you think of Malcolm X's "A Homemade Education." It's at minimum one of the knife-edges of hope and anger for a whole generation, regarding the promise and disappointment of the Nelson Mandela revolution.

Unathi Slasha grew up here. He's not from Wakanda.

He was one of the two-standout students in the M.A. in Creative Writing program at Rhodes University where I was the Mellon Scholar. We performed at the National Arts Festival. His writing embodies some of the major tendencies in emergent African writing today: a blend of folklore, internal psychological crisis, a dash of genre (crime especially) and a political call to action that is as much a call to heart as it to arms. He's precisely part of his time. But he doesn't stop there.

When the Nigerian Amos Tutuola broke through with *The Palm Wine Drinkard* and *My Life in the Bush of Ghosts*, the entire reading world took notice. If you have the smartest French people on the planet and Dylan Thomas behind you, you don't need anyone else. Suddenly, people began to grasp the incredible riches of Yoruba culture that were already out there...in the Americas and the Caribbean...the UK...all of Europe.

Slasha now offers us the new Afro hip-hop Xhosa version of the Tutuola Reset.

He's the full "man of letters"...critic, editor, performer, as well as author. In his home country he gets exactly the kind of snarky snubs from the prim and jealous that is the one sure sign of getting somewhere. At some point in the future, I'm going to be in a grand city like New York or London, and he'll be very famous. I have faith in his magic to sense my presence and to yell out over all the tabloid heads and noise. We're all tired and done with "writing" and literature. It's blood magic or nothing now. My favorite genius, and I've earned the gunshot right to say that.

—Kris Saknussemm, author of Private Midnight

SWARTKOPS AND SOMAGWAZA

There is a well in this bush. It's known as Swartkops. Origin of the name is still being disputed throughout Khayamnandi Township. Some say it was coined by Somagwaza. Others argue that it's untrue, that it could not have been him. Only certain abakhwetha with the birthmark of Somagwaza are able to hear the rushing waters during the day and the freezing stillness of the well during the night. It is not known who named the well and when. My uncle, Naliti, is amongst those who hold this belief with an unshakable conviction.

Certain nights, Naliti says, the moonlight projects onto the waters the image of an old woman carrying the baldhead of Somagwaza. Nobody sees the image and lives long. Naliti claims to be the only Man who has seen the baldhead and managed to reverse the curse. He never tells what he did to dodge the seventh day curse.

During my childhood nights, heard Father and Naliti talk about this matter. Their faces were always darkened with seriousness. They spoke about this again during my adult life. Though some parts of the story were missing or altered, their facial expressions remained stern as ever. On crescent moonlit nights, Naliti claims, the waters of the well are clean. Not salty and littered like the Perseverance River's, which is becoming a hostile habitat for water animals. Feet have travelled and circled the bush, hands digging wild potatoes and hunting beasts, more than once. Never have I come across a well here in Kwafindoda.

Sun has been sitting still in the middle of the sky, staring and pouring down yellow heat, the entire week. Each boring day, ibhuma lam turns into a furnace. Soil is hot. Roasts my soles as they touch the ground. The way things look, the sail of ibhuma is going to melt. Everything has been quietened by the heat. Trees are all dead still. Birds are nestled quietly on the branches of the tall tree I've named. Inhale the hotness of the day. Scorches my nostrils and chest as I breathe. The way my eyes burn and itch to bleed I have no idea what's holding them from raining blood. Keep my eyes closed. Lie on my back on my bedding.

Try to adjust the pace of my breathing. The quicker I breathe the more searing the activity becomes. Slow my breathing down. Heave, inflate my chest. Push out a breath in the softest manner I can manage. Open my eyes after the burning has lessened. Must get used to enduring the caustic experience of breathing while I wait for my eyes to cool down.

Slightly open my eyes. Stare at the opening in the roof of ibhuma. Irregular sheets of heat fall down to sear my brown skin to charcoal. Grown lazy to smear ingceke on my skin. Naliti has told me that it's protective against hotness and wicked spirits. Can't bear the time consuming chore of smearing it on my body. Shift. Position myself to lie on my left hand side. Look into the distance through a cut in the sail. Heat, from a distance, resembles an oasis. Glows like sand in the sun, giving me the impression of a well. Ignore this image.

If I were as gullible as Kwafindoda thinks, I would crawl out of ibhuma and run after this image of water. Getting accustomed to the mirages of this bush. Heat does not hurt my skin the way it does when I walk about under this exhausting sun. Safer to be in one place, sit still or lie on my back when the heat makes it hard for me to breathe. This is especially important since I go about day and night un-ngceke-ed.

Shut my eyes and imagine myself immersed in Swartkops' fresh and sweet water. Smile as I think of how I would not hesitate to jump in and bathe for the longest time, as if to taunt the forever sweltering sun, not caring about the results of my actions. Would not go out of the water til I witnessed my legs stitch themselves into a fish tail.

Being roasted in this heat is a language of Kwafindoda, telling me that the well has been burnt out of existence.

Swartkops and Somagwaza have never existed, says the heat.

Thick and black sail of ibhuma absorbs and traps this unbearable hotness to harden my flesh. Heat has dried my skin and eyes. Hard and sore, as are the tips of my fingers. Almost impossible to keep my eyes open for long. Fear they will burst and bleed from the intensity of this ungodly heat.

Heat heightens the rotten smell of isinyenye. Froths,

yellow fluid drips, ityeba loosens a bit. Inhale the rottenness and feel like am going to throw up. Doubt it. Won't
vomit, have not eaten since I can no longer remember
when. Dizzying sensation remains in my gut. Won't go
outside ibhuma in this punishing heat. But the nausea
grabs my neck and drives me out. Want relief. Need
saving from both the heat and the stinking smell arising
from between my thighs. Don't know how many times I
have been washing umthondo. Stubborn smell remains,
even after several soft scrubs and exposure of my crotch
to the afternoon breeze.

Outside. Sit in the shade of krwecizulu. My legs wide
open. Back rests against the bark. Sharp smell jumps up
and lingers inside my nostrils, giddying my head. No
nausea. Feel extremely hungry I could, in no time, kill,
peel and gobble down the first mouse or rabbit I come
across. Stomach winds and whirls painfully, intent on
curling my intestines into a tie. Think of the traps I've
knotted and plotted around ibhuma. Why is it so hard to
catch a springbok or a kudu or a buck or a damn hare in
this bush, even with the trickiest of snares I learned from
Naliti?

Yesterday, I collapsed while chasing a buck. Or maybe I
imagined that it was a buck as, out of desperation, I had
found myself stuffing my mouth with magic mushrooms. The thing was agile. Tried catching up with the
speed of this shadowy buck. My chest heated. I could
hardly breathe. Head was preparing to explode. I could
feel the stinging pain of the thorns impaled into my
soles. Still feel the pain in the form of needles pricking
my heart. When I walk, I tread softly. What did I expect?

Can't be running around in the punishing sun, in a body freed of the heaviness of ifutha.

That shadowy buck sprang in various directions, hurrying, confusing me so much I could not stand still and aim my arrow. Now it was here, the next moment it was springing further, covering large distances. Followed it closely. Behind umnga tree, I stood and waited for it to tire. I had no such luck. Beast disappeared into the bushes while I was preparing to shoot it. Disappointment I felt afterwards weighed me down and collapsed my body and brain.

Stand up and walk towards my traps, although I know checking them is a waste of time. If my booby traps had caught an animal, the beast would have told me by screaming its pain. Here are fresh tracks of a springbok. Beast was clever enough to dodge its death. Saw the trap and jumped over it. How angering! How did it discover it? I've placed and covered the traps with iingcongolo! My chest deflates with irritation. Sure enough, the other traps have caught nothing. Disappointment cuts through me. This time, it only weakens my limbs.

Fall to the ground; squat for a while. It's a shame that there are lots of roaming animals here, yet they never bother walking into my traps, even though I have ensured that the traps are invisible to these beasts of Kwafindoda. Look around. There are tracks all over. All the trees' leaves and branches are still.

Tread back to sit in the shade of the tall tree. Watch a group of flies feeding on the rotten crap I dropped a while back. Listen to the noise of my stomach while fighting off the suffocating heat by adjusting my breathing pattern. Flies glide in a black wave towards me. Buzz annoyingly. Break off a krwecizulu branch;

whack the flies away. Stubborn and refuse to leave me alone. These tiny bastards want to congregate on my crotch! Break off another branch and cover my crotch, careful not to prod isinyenye. Keep whacking the little shits away til they can't take it anymore. Finally, they give up and go back to hover over my black crap.

Think of my brother, inqalathi. Why has he not delivered imvotho and iwaba lam? Has something happened to him on his way to me? Or has Father commanded him to stop delivering ukumunda and imvotho to me? Why did not they tell me about their decision when they were here? If this is one of the ways of making me a Man, then it is a sick and selfish custom. They should have told me that there was going to be a time when I was going to be forced to fend for myself.

Wonder if Father knows that the beasts here are smart enough to sniff out danger and escape. Don't know how long I've waited to encounter another animal so as to make use of my weapon. If I see one I will definitely hit it flat with my poisoned arrow. Learned this tactic from Naliti. He handed me this weapon and showed me uncwadi the plant whose utywala can be used for blades. My arrowheads sleep in this sap. If I shoot and hit a beast, its muscles will weaken and the beast will collapse in a drunken state. Have not seen this happen yet. Have not encountered another beast, ever since that buck.

Get up. Look at the pathway that leads to ebuhlanti. Narrow; only one person can manoeuvre along it at a time. Plod softly on the footpath. Pass the boundary that I should not cross because it is said that this will affect my wellbeing. Have jumped over this black waterfilled trench more than a thousand times and nothing has happened to me. More I desire cooked or roasted meat, the more the urge to run into ebuhlanti to grab a chicken or drag a sheep intensifies.

Want to look into the township. Maybe I will see inqalathi hurrying from a distance. All I have been doing here is stand on this mound and study the shepherd. Have memorised his daily duties and mastered his words. Can tell his laugh from that of his friends. They only visit him on Friday afternoons for a drink of iBheya. Right after the white van arrives. They help the driver offload the two tanks of clean water, one is carried inside the cabin, and the other is emptied into the long bathtub ebuhlanti.

I know the exact time he leaves his cabin and the moment of his return. Last time I saw his girlfriend in the cabin's yard, he was swearing and shouting and spitting and, intermittently, picking up stones and casting them at her. S'fombo was drunk. She was sober. After dodging the cast stones, she reached S'fombo. Grabbed him by his chestflesh. They struggled. She poured out a vicious torrent of blows. Stream of blows and klaps kept up with his swearing motormouth. He kept shouting, Sund'bamba, njakazi, ndiyeke, msunu ka nyoko, ndiyeke! and did nothing else but thwack his tongue against his palate. S'fombo's girlfriend enjoyed beating poor S'fombo, as much as he enjoyed swearing and receiving blows and klaps. She punched his throat thrice. He vomited on her white blouse. Collapsed. All of these details I know. Can recite o' by heart. But how are they helpful to me when they cannot kill my hunger and thirst?

On the mound. The palm tree overlooks my head. It's

said to have been around here since way back, but has never borne a single fruit. Naliti knows everything. He told me that this tree was cursed to barrenness. But he has never revealed to me the identity of this person who cursed it. I like the tree because it shelters me from the confrontational sun whenever I want to enjoy the view.

Township looks tiny from where am standing. Antlike heads walk the streets. Can't even say that one of the heads is inqalathi. They walk back and forth, up and down, in those streets. Streets do not get empty. None of these heads come my way. What a horrible experience! Can't even shout to them to go tell inqalathi to bring ibhekile nemvotho. Truth is, even if I were to shout, body would collapse right after the activity. Sun's hotness will not allow me to shout without falling $at on my face. Even so, doubt those tiny heads would be able to hear my raspy and tired voice. Dehydration and hunger are giving me a hard time. Can feel dizziness surging, hellbent on choking me unconscious. Throat is as dry and hard as the parched soil under my cracked heels. Refuse to resort to drinking the salty water of the Perseverance River or the muddy black water in the trench.

Cows and sheep and chickens are quiet ebuhlanti. Paying attention to the deafening heat; their bodies deadened and numbed. S'fombo is in the shade of the big tree, lying on a dirty and torn mattress.

He gets up, his skin sweaty and sticky. Limps into his cabin. Returns naked from the waist up. Carries a grimy bucket filled with water. Bits of water spill over as he struggles towards ebuhlanti. Opens the gate, enters. If I get a chance. I'll run into ebuhlanti. Drink the water. Slaughter the chickens. I'll host a oneman meat carnival ebhumeni. But S'fombo has been quite vigilant lately. I know why this is so. He has not been seeing his girl-friend. She lives in Sakkiesdorp.

Last night, he locked the cabin and tied his bulldog to the gate of his yard, to guard ubuhlanti. I know those black pigs ebuhlanti are hair-raising, but that bulldog is the scariest, with its dripping jaws, a big and wide croc-odile mouth and tough teeth. May be scared of the dog, but it would never defeat me. My thirst and hunger are stronger than it! I was about to risk it and go down. Beat the dog to death with ikrali. Sneak into ebuhlanti. But S'fombo quickly returned. It was as though he had had a premonition.

Stand on the mound and watch S'fombo. He's back on his mattress, battling a group of flies, buzzing and irritating his face. He catches some with his palm; tosses them in his toothless mouth. He is sick, I think. What is he doing? How does a fly taste? Meat or mushrooms? Study his behaviour closely. Want to see if there are any changes after he has eaten a handful of huge flies. Nothing odd happens to S'fombo. He is just as fine as ever.

Think for a long time. Should I eat flies, or should I wait longer til S'fombo leaves his cabin and go get myself chickens from ebuhlanti? Weigh all available sides. Turn around and tiptoe back. Each step I take equals my soles being knifed. Refuse to focus on the pain of it. If I grab an army of flies am sure it will sustain me till the next day. Losing faith in inqalathi, in hunting; doesn't help me in any way. Think about the flies. Nobody will know that I have eaten flies. The starved have no shame. Remember the words of Naliti and stick to my decision to catch and eat flies.

Walk towards krwecizulu to check for the flies. Sun has travelled across the sky. No longer standing in the middle. Even the air is no longer as intensely dry and hot as it was earlier in the day. My crap has darkened and hardened into a spiral roll. Flies have flown. Nowhere near the shit. Angering! Should not have wasted time thinking about the dangers of eating flies. Should have gone back to the flies hovering over my crap right after seeing S'fombo swallow flies. Certain they don't taste bad. Don't know why am being choosey. Used to feasting on shanks and feet soup – the most disgusting meal I have ever encountered! Gap in my stomach widens. Think about the flies, their taste and how they would have made a difference, no matter how little. Maybe there is a way to eating flies. Did not notice whether S'fombo chewed or swallowed. Maybe the juice that exploded and flooded his mouth as he crunched the bodies of the flies is enjoyable, if those tiny frames contain any juice at all.

Lying on my bedding, its hardness hurts my back. Bedding is the worst, but a man has to go through all kinds of hardships. Otherwise, what is the point of having ijwabi sliced, being obliged to build ibhuma on my own while isinyenye pains? Blankets are drenched in lice and ticks. Suck and bite – bloody parasites! Sit up straight. Grab and roll the blankets into a bundle.

Toss it to the corner on my right. Getting used to my own bodily rottenness. Naliti told me this is my first house, my first yard and a Man knots his responsibilities to his belt. Nobody else is going to feed me. Must get up and fend for food. For now, I have to let my body rest. But the hunger does not want me to rest. Twist and turn as I try to lie on my back on these cardboards. Although they are rough and uncomfortable, it is much better than being covered in blankets that suck and bite my body and plague my skin with scars and callouses! Shift my body, trying to find a relaxed position that will not hurt me. After much restlessness, rest on my right hand side. Look through the peephole, the trees are now calm and cool. Afternoon. Wave their branches, shed their leaves at will. Close my eyes. Imagine I have discovered sweet Swartkops. All my traps have caught beasts.

EMZINI OBOMVU

S'fombo comes out of his cabin, carrying a waterfilled waskom. He topples it, emptying the water onto his lawn. He's dressed in his khaki clothes and black boots. I've been watching him the entire day, from the mound, under the palm tree. He has been acting unusual, doing things outside his habits. He's confused, thinking about his girlfriend.

Glad the sun did not show me flames. Heat has been moderate since dawn. Spent half this morning sitting still in the shade of this cursed palm tree til I got tired of inactivity. Tread down the narrow pathway, heading towards the prickly pear tree. Near it and step much closer for observation.

Last week, the prickly pear tree was bare. Now, it's densely leaved and heavily hung with fat fruits. Pluck and eat a few prickly pears though it's still very unclear as to how the fruits of this tree have grown so fast and big. Help myself on the fruits til I feel it is enough.

Naliti said I should not eat lots of prickly pears.

When I asked him why not, he chuckled, said: Awuyazi? Yintoni engaziyo, mkhwetha?

Walk back to my chilling spot near the palm tree. Day has begun declining into dusk. A gentle wind tickles my eyes; become watery as I unblinkingly watch S'fombo. He's about to go out. He locks his cabin but forgets to lock his gate. He walks out his yard built of iron sheets, treads towards the township, and disappears beyond the corroded shipping containers, broken-down, rusted old cars that flank the footpath that leads into Khayamnandi.

Rush down into ebuhlanti. Cattle shriek, bustling about. The lamb and the sheep cuddle at the corner, frightened into frozen figures. A group of cows come running towards me. Sidestep. They hit their heads against the metal gate, drop on their backs and dangle their dirty tongues. Chickens screech frantically, flaking and filling ubuhlanti with feathers. Pigeons take o' from the earth, leaving droppings as they fly into the sky, warming their bodies in the sun. Highpitched moos of the cows cut in correctly every time the chickens take a brief break from squeaking.

Grab a fat, redfurred chicken. Throttle its throat with my right hand. It kicks, scratches my chest and hands with its claws. It squeaks. Squeeze its neck harder between my forefinger and thumb til the sound ceases. Life escapes. Mngqundu! Deliver a hefty kick to the barking bulldog at the gate. It squeals and hobbles in the direction of the township –a threelegged cripple.

I have eaten one lamb and a few chickens. S'fombo hasn't asked me about the missing animals. I doubt he suspects me. Not allowed to go down from ibhuma to ebuhlanti.

When I asked my uncle, Naliti, who's been instilling me with isidoda, why am not allowed to go stand on the mound near ebuhlanti, to look into the township, he replied: Kwakunje kwatanci, kwantlandlolo — sisidoda eso, ndoqa!

Thick fog falls, drags along the ground. Birds screech from the wavering trees. They flap their wings, fall, break necks and die before my feet. Kick a dead bird and it flies and hits another bird that perches on a branch of krwecizulu. Can't be eating birds that I have not killed myself. Naliti said doing that will anger the ancestors, and they will make sure that isinyenye does not heal.

Rush up the filthstrewn footpath to ibhuma, holding the chicken. Clear my way with my panga. Not carrying ikrali. Face and body haven't seen ingceke for over a week. If Father or ikhankatha catch me like this, they'll punish me greatly.

Stealing is better than waiting for food to be brought by that little brat, my brother. He doesn't even bring ibhekile yam, he goes to the drain pipes with his friends to eat my food and play around before going home to refill it. Only to go back to the drain pipes and eat my food again.

See him hurrying home, swinging ibhekile and tossing it emoyeni only to catch it before it falls. Shout til my voice is hoarse, waving ikrali, whistling his name in vain. Decide if am going to rely on that brat, I will die from hunger and thirst.

Night is riotous. Whirlwind draws into its centre all the debris of dust, dregs of rubbish near it. Fear for ibhuma.

It will be blown away easily. Wisdom of the elders, which claims this wobbly thing is my first house, will not hold it together through the imminent storm.

Kneel, crawl into ibhuma. Gather bits of wood and plastic bags and squash them into a bundle. Sprinkle paraffin over the bundle and light the thing. Burns. Feed the weak fire with more plastic bags and papers. Choke and cough and my eyes burn from the gust of black smoke til I get hiccups.

Cannot understand why I don't hear the beating and slashing of the wind against the sail. Burn a fistful of impepho; inhale its sharp whiff hoping the irritating hiccups die. Strike a matchstick, light the paraffined bundle once more, but it dies again. Run out of matches to reignite it. Blades of hunger have begun chopping my innards. Can't wait to roast this chicken.

Crawl outside to get stones. Pick up four flat pebbles, but they are all wet from the dew and fog. Doubt they will do the job. Remember that last night I left a lighter in one of the gourds near the river. Throw the pebbles away. Sling my bag over my shoulder and slide the panga kwisingxobo sayo. Head eastward. So foggy I can't see my hand.

Last night, when I came from bathing my crotch, something said I should paint certain stones and trees along the sideway. Pathway is now riddled with dead birds and pigeons. They all died the same way, their bodies petrified and mouths overflowing with ubuxhwangu namaphela.

Sky is a black cloak stitched together by lightning. Cracks and crashes of thunder fill my heart and head with throbs and fright. Body quivers and gets rocky with goosebumps.

I know Kwafindoda like Jah knows the number of my hairs on my head. They have grown so long over the past month. It's like this in Kwafindoda. You get to experience all kinds of unusual sounds, all kinds of unusual fauna and flora boys know nothing about and have never seen. I know herbs, I know plants, I know flowers, and I know animals and insects. Pass all the painted landmarks.

Look around for edible blackberries, prickly pears or sour figs to rid my stomach of making noise and farting. Prickly pear tree is entirely plucked. There isn't a single fruit around on the ground. One of Mthimkhulu's tricks. He likes doing that when he's bored. But it's so odd. Why would he do it during a whirlwind night?

Dip my forefinger into the black mud. Make a cross sign on my forehead. Wait for the thing to dry. Pick a flat stone, toss it into the waters. Cross Perseverance River, treading on the stones that are placed two steps apart. Watchful of the alligators and crocodiles that are baring their dripping jaws out of the muddy waters. On the other side, I slide through huge trees, thicket and stumps. Hard feet cut through rubble and foliage. Perseverance River glows in the fog. Opposite the mouth of Perseverance River is the cave in which Mthimkhulu lives.

I shout:

Ek sê Mthi!

Voice echoes in the caverns of the cave. No response. Kneel. Crawl into the cave. Place where he sleeps is empty. His belongings are not here. Crawl out and begin to look for the gourd with the lighter.

At the edges of the river, there are white and black lilies decorating the transparent water. All the creatures swim back and forth. Naliti once told me that I shouldn't drink this salty water lest I get sick with stomach ulcers and die. Drawn to take o' isibheshu and jump into the water. Perseverance River seduces me when I stare into it. Take the lighter from the gourd. Find my way back.

Get to the fifth landmark, which is a stone that bears my nickname, JAH HILLS, in big ingceke marks. It has been shifted. The JAH has been blackened with dark blood. Panic, but I keep walking. From a short distance, ibhuma is visible.

Get to the last landmark, which is twenty-five steps away from ibhuma. It begins to rain, gets windy. Whirlwind is nearing. Beer cans and stones and plastics and papers and broken tree branches and foliage $ y around in circles in the sky.

Underneath my feet, the earth is wet and soft. Shivers and exhales a great steam of thick smoke. Whirlwind. Vacuums everything it can to become bigger, belligerent – almost like it's morphing into a storm. Trees sway like haywire kites. Animals and birds are terrified to death. Naliti did warn me about the haunting oddities of Kwafindoda. Hope akhomntu uphazamise ubuthongo beNkanyamba, or refused the seduction of Mamlambo emlanjeni.

This other night, I watched a woman bathe and brush her long hair by the waters. She turned her head around, but could not look me in the eyes. My face was bright with ifutha. Watched her cupping and pouring water onto her breasts down to her vagina. Felt umthondo bulging with lust. Felt tempted to wash ingceke o' my

face, but thought hard about the tough burden of
fucking with umthondo obuhlungu and sneaked away
instead.

Struggle through the thorn bushes, bruising my
thighs, legs, hands, face. Strands of my bushy hair and
pieces of my flesh are left on the thorns. Wind bites my
skin with its sharp teeth. Feet are riddled with ameva.
Bear the pain of it all hoping to reach ibhuma. Heard
stories of hunters and herbgatherers who were swallowed and swirled and su'ocated to death in the whirlwind. Surprised that, in these conditions, ibhuma hasn't
been uprooted and swept away by the storm.

Ten black and white figures. Hover around ibhuma,
humming and flapping their wings, eyelashes in a crazy
way. Their presences light up my enclosure. Lightning
draws, in the black sky, a figure of a giant bird. Opens its
hooked beak. Lightning bursts.

Come closer and they turn their backs. Stand near
krwecizulu, my heart beating fast, fear mounting my
chest and making me feel like am going to choke.
Huntshu! I shout, waving my panga. MaTshawe! Finger
the rhino horn on my necklace. Creatures stop flapping
their wings. Turn around. Stare at me. Eyes empty, dark.
Rumbling and lightning in my enclosure halts. Bodies
are glowing embers. They drop down on the ground,
walk into the thicket and disappear. My enclosure
dissolves back into its dark, foggy state.

Gather plastics, cardboards, wood sticks and crunch
them into a bundle. Sprinkle para& n. Light the wet
thing. Shove my hand under my bedding; pull out my
butcher knife. Stained with blackened blood.

At the corner, I cannot find the pot that contains my chicken. Notice ingceke yam has been spilled – now mixed with soil.

Under my wooden headrest, I cannot find the bag that contains ubumdaka bam. Panic. Sit on my bedding. Take a dry skin layer of an onion. Take out the ganja. Swaai a thick zol, light it and begin smoking, blowing out smoke. Draws itself into different figures, which are all birds, animals, faces.

Outside, cracks of laughter roar. Echo diminishes, disappears into the other side of Kwafindoda. Noises of the bush, here, cats cry childrenlike and baboons scream humanlike. Noises return in a blasting sound. Hands scrape and search the ground, grab the plastic with herbs, burn a bigger bundle of impepho and finish o' the zol.

At the door, the head of my dead chicken stands on its now elongated beak. A crowd of mosquitoes and flies hover behind the head in great rage. The head springs toward me, poking about with its beak, seeking my crotch. I jump up, swaying and dodging its stings. We carry on like this til the chicken head becomes red and begins to shriek.

Its body jumps inside, stands next to the head, and its feet make jerky movements. The head stops shrieking. It thrusts twice into the ground. The mosquitoes and flies come to me in the figure of a knife. Stagger up, strike the side sail of ibhuma open with my Okapi, and jump out. The chicken head, its body and the mosquitoes and flies are after me. Bump into bushes and branches. Jump through hedges and hillocks, striking aimlessly with my panga, screaming: MaTshawe! MaTshawe!

Hide behind krwecizulu. Inside, the spirits are hissing things I can't know. Regret not asking Naliti how to decode their whisperings. Maybe they want to warn me and advise me on how to escape this danger. Watch the chicken head, its body and the mosquitoes and flies madly searching for me in the fog. They are joined by a goat. Resembles the one I roasted and ate at umojiso. Should have chopped its skin and o'al into pieces, burned them and thrown the ashes into the river. Instead, I buried them. Skin is now stuffed. Looks bloodless.

The head (carelessly sewn back onto the stuffed skin) blinks thrice every minute. Rotates in a robotic way. Rub the rhino horn with my palm. On the ground, near the grotesque roots of krwecizulu, a black woodpecker winces, writhes in the dust, trying to free its body and beak from spiderwebs. Rolls on its stomach, begins to beat its body against my heel. Beak picks at my big toe. Pick up the bird, free its body and beak. Chirps, jumps up and down and pees on my palm.

Steal my way through the bushes, panga charting out a new pathway. Bird follows me, flying close to my left ear, lighting with its big, bright eyes. Light from its eyes orbits in balls that cut clear through the fog. Feel better with this bird beside me. Hope Mthimkhulu is back in his cave. He's the only person that can help me in Kwafindoda, now that I haven't seen my brother, inqalathi. Have no idea why Father hasn't been visiting.

Last time I saw Father and Naliti was the morning after umojiso. They were so stuffed on the goat meat and drunk on umqombothi and whisky. They began fighting over who had met Somagwaza first and whose ibhuma had burnt last. Choke on a chuckle as I remember how Father wanted to stickfight with Naliti, although he knew his obesity would not allow him to win.

Should have followed the example of my big brother and gone to build ibhuma in the little bush in Sakkiesdorp. Father told me that wasn't going to happen. He told me a real man goes to Kwafindoda and survives alone til the elders decide that he has learnt to be a Man.

Twenty years ago, when my big brother returned from Zanempilo, there were only family and church members' emgidini wakhe. Townships refuse to attend imigidi of boys who've been made men at the Zanempilo clinic. Father ordered Mother to take away and lock all the cases of soft drinks in the storeroom. He said he wanted my younger brother and me to go to Kwafindoda.

Mthimkhulu's cave is still empty. Gather bits of wood that are lying around, set them alight. The hunger pain coils my intestines into a knot. Look at this thick bird and think about all the good reasons not to snap its neck and roast it on this weak fire. It stares at me innocently. Decide to let the thought of killing it go. Isinyenye itches as I think about my bag that contains ubumdaka bam. It's one of Mthi's sick tricks, reminding me that am in Kwafindoda.

Half asleep, cuddled at the corner. Fire dances to death. Embers turn black. Bird snores, blowing out tiny bubbles of mucus through its nose. Reflection of the moon, on the river, shoots shafts of light into this side of the cave. Think of food and yawn.

Get on my knees, peep through a hole. Night is pale with fog. Finger the rhino horn. Fog comes down like thick slices of white bread, one on top of another. No, the fog crumbles down like huge balls of umphokoqo. It's annoying to picture all the nourishing food I can't have.

Sigh, sit ngeempundu. My face lightens upon seeing a platter of roasted chicken breast, lamb legs sitting on the ashes. Jump to my feet. Oh maTshawe amahle! Don't care how it got here. Stretch my arm, reach for the platter. In no time, I finish o' the chicken, and then I begin stuffing myself with titbits of the lamb.

Gather all the meat bones and stand up. Throw them out the hole. On the far corner of the cave there is ibhekile boiling, brimming with umdoko. Khawuta! Tshiwo! Nkosi yam! Don't care how it got here. Briskly reach for it. Drink umdoko in three gulps. Put ibhekile down, lean ngeempundu against the jutting stone behind me.

A sound of drums erupts. Muffled voices, humming and laughter join the outburst. They are silenced, only to come back in a loud blast. Din wakes the bird. Stunned. Ruffes its wings, hovers near the exit, lighting the way.

Crawl out, my mouth shouts: Mthi, mfethu!

The outburst seems to arise from inside the caverns of the cave. Or maybe it's an echo from the depth of the bush. At the mouth of the river, a woman plays naked in the sand. She sees me, smiles, beckons me forth with her thin fingers. Bird pecks at my cheek. Flies in front of my face, chirping, flustering its wings as though imploring me not to go to her. Cannot fight the seductive beauty. Her sagging yellow breasts bulge umthondo, veins thump and isinyenye itches. Her face is round, ravishingly scarified. Her eyes, golden fireballs. Look deep into them. Am in her retina, brushing her cheeks, hair, sticking my tongue into her round mouth.

She lies on her back on the sand. Bird has flown away. Woman parts her thighs. She closes her eyes. Recall what Naliti once told me of how as umkhwetha he fucked a womanfish. Naliti gave me a short stick of umlomo omnandi and told me if I ever meet a woman near the river, I must seduce and fuck her to test umthondo. But isinyenye has not fully healed but this does not stop me.

Get closer to her. My hands touch her breasts. Fingers fondle her dark nipples. Lick her chin. Put my mouth around her nose; poke the tip of my tongue in her left nostril, in her right nostril, the tip keeps changing holes. She moans and seems to like it this way.

She lays spread out on the sand. Minc' iintsula, press my weight against her yellow body. My open palms pin her hands on the sand. She pushes her crotch towards me. Thi-xo wam, I say, as I thrust. Pleasure yebhentse yakhe surges in me. Poke umthondo in and out, each turn digging deep in the different corners yebhentse. Her eyeballs roll in a crazy rotation. She makes guttural noises. She punches my chest, pushes her crotch forth in fast motions. Grind and gyrate.

She gasps. My toes sink into the sand. Stroke once, suddenly dic. Numbness. Not surprised – have not fucked in six months. Her hips are still in a fucking rage, though umthondo has weakened, balls shrivelled. Woman stops, sits ngeempundu. She grimaces, brings up her tiny hand, strikes me across my face. Look at her. She spits into my mouth. Her spit is sour, it burns my tongue. She rubs my balls in her hand. Her rough palm irritably tickles me. Nauseated by her sour spit, I push her off me. She falls on her back, rumbles, Ndizeke kakuhle!

Umthondo wam ubuhlungu, I tell her, as I sit ngeempundu and nurse isinyenye.

Ndizeke ngoku kwedini! she shouts. Her eyes turn red and her body shivers.

She turns around, kneels. Iimpundu are impressively big and beautiful. Umthondo bulges and thumps. Slips into her moist pussy. Drive it in and out. It feels good, yet painful. Forget about isinyenye. Wetness seeps, circles my waist. Shove umthondo deep ebhentseni yakhe, my hands holding, parting her butt cheeks. Move slowly this time. No more fast strokes, isinyenye singavuleka. She moans, punches the sand. Cut open deep holes. Her body trembles as iintsula zakhe loosen and shake jellylike. Her black locs harden, wooden sticks, growing from her head. Feel a sharp cut emthondweni.

Suyeka! Her harsh voice threatens me. Pull umthondo out. Hold it in my palm. Drenched in blood, isinyenye siyaphefumla. Thumps with a fierce stinging. Fall ngeempundu, nurse umthondo. Take isibheshu off, wipe the blood. Try bandaging it with a cloth. But the woman distracts me. Beats my arms, prods my head.

Ndizeke ngoku wena! Her voice is hoarse and her tone spells irritation.

Turn my head and say, Awuboni ndibuhlungu?

She strikes the back of my head with something

sharp. Bleed, stagger to my feet, fumbling for my panga, but it's nowhere in my possession. Her legs have become two huge, thick, slithering snakes.

Ha, ha, ha, ha, ha! Ucimba ndinguMamlambo! Unyile! she says meanly.

Her face changes. She appears like Nomali, my dead girlfriend's mother, and then she resembles Mandy's father, Phung' Amanzi. Snakes disengage from her body, sink into the sand. Skulk towards me. Before I can dash out of her sight, the snakes have reached me. Coil themselves up my legs. One of them, the big-headed one, tickles my balls with its flickering tongue. Weaken me with their venomous breath, squeezing my body til it's emptied of energy. Glide back to her.

She regains her two legs. Walks towards me. Grabs and drags me to the mouth of the river. Shoves my head into the water. Keeps it there for some time. Hold my breath til my head feels like bursting. She pulls my head out, drags me by my legs, corners me against a jutting stone of the cave. Kicks my ribs, punches my face, pushes me around. Roll, my back scrapes against a stone. Moan. She laughs. But her laugh is a shriek. She releases the snakes again. They sneak around to taunt me with their tongues.

My ears drip discharge. Snakes lick the fluid. The read of sticky substance runs rounds on my body. Hovering, she shoves a fist in her vagina, pulls out a bag. Out the bag, a bottled red powder. Holds my head, sprinkling the powder in my face, says: Emzini Obomvu.

BHAKUBHA

Find myself trapped inside a container made of flesh. Long and short pipes run over my head. Flesh-container leaks mucus, slime, all kinds of gluey liquids. Hold my breath. Clamp my mouth with my palm. Head and body aches. Rancid smell cuts through my palm. Holding my breath does not help. Vomit. Something from underneath my feet cracks its lips. Receives the vomit. Mouth closes.

On the roof of this flesh-container, a skin cracks open. Arise and drift in the air with pasty liquids, filthy bones and animal skulls. Opening sucks, swallows me only to spew me out. Land on my back, hi! ing my head hard on the red gravel road. Lucky – my small head does not break in half. Dizzy, sticky. Shake my head. Water mixed with blood shoots out my mouth and ears. Summon tears to wash the vagueness out of my eyes.

Daylight. Sky is silver, air is arid. Stomach hurts from the smells. Dead things – foul fish, putrid pigs and decayed dogs. Along the roadside rubbish and corpses are piled up in heaps. Insects, three-headed dogs have their necks buried in the mess. These little boys, with dead eyes, who are supposed to play amaqhina or cumbelele or iceya, splash in the putrid black water in a ditch, sling heads and toes of corpses at one another. Prove Mother wrong – a rubbish dump for human beings exists.

Fo-fo-llow me, the woman stammers. She leads the way, and my legs limp behind. Surprised that she addresses me in English. She looks very different; hair is locked, bright red.

She points her index finger to the sky, says, We have to get to the house before the last heave. Her eyes twinkle with excitement.

Walk through a mob of people. Those who are bald have plastered their faces with red ochre. Its dry-ness makes their faces look like fissured red earth. Assume this is a market. Old women flash ugly teeth and lick their cracked lips. Wave at me from behind their fast-food and vegetable-stalls. Teeth are grey, tongues white. Wrinkled hands cup their baggy breasts, wink at me. Old men limp, stumble on yellow stones scattered on the road. Stop and look at me with swollen faces, flattened eyes as though they pity me. Young boys walk about selling plastic bags of black corn and bottles of aphro-disiac concoction. Four chained young men, dragged by two old women, wave weakly. Open their mouths. Loud sound blasts. Group of women at the corner, sit t ing on tree stumps, overtone-singing, jump to their feet, clasp their hands.

Rrrr----rush nnnn---now, says the Stammerer.

Want to laugh at how she speaks. Is she making this entire stammering thing up? Drag my hurting feet along the red gravel road. Seems to lead to a white-roofed red house ahead. Pass the Liquor Store built of thatch. At the door there's a line of people holding cups and jugs, waiting their turn to get in. A naked boy runs out holding a cup, spilling bits of the red liquid on the red earth, shouting, Yippy, yippy! Face of the boy sickens me. Wrenches my intestines for he resembles my brother so well. Miss my brother, with his long face, his loud and lousy laugh. Boy disappears behind the Medicine Shop, but the image of his face remains in my mind. Throat itches. Cough. Stomach and heart are noisy.

Trudge through the vast plantation, passing rows of pumpkins and potatoes and tomatoes and cabbages and spinaches and black corn and oranges. Feel tiny beings running up my legs licking and biting me. Stand still for a moment. Try shaking these insects off my legs. As soon as the biting sensation subsides, I continue following the footsteps of the Stammerer. Nobody is talking to nobody. Stammerer hardly stops to look back to check if am still behind her. A person could easily ambush her and thrash her out of her wits. That person is definitely not me.

Plod along rows of big plastic tanks that contain rain water. Looking at the hungry faces of the people we pass sitting alongside the road, hope this is not how I get eaten here. Watched a movie like that once, and the kidnapped girl had to choose between slaving and being supper.

Red house is surrounded by blue huts. It overlooks the black sea which spews out dead crabs and fishes every time it crashes against the jutting rocks. Hyenas and lions move around with corpses clenched and hanging between their dripping jaws. At the metal gate is a dreadlocked woman crouching in the sky. Her elephantine body is supported by locs that are erect like pillars. Woman's locs are long. Drag on the ground. Some twist and turn in the sky like snakes. Others spread out from her head to make a net enclosing the red building. Next to her snores a cat the size of a hyena. Cat is white with reddish spots that expand and contract as it inhales and exhales gusts of black smoke through its nostrils.

Twice this week, mhmm? Dreadlocked woman's voice is thin and soft – it would not scare away a cockroach. She touches one of her locs, the gate slides open. She sneezes, spittle sticks onto my face. Stammerer nods, says something in a language I don't understand. Loud sigh of the sea sounds again. Sky slowly darkens. Yellow patches on the small cracked cloud. It has been floating and keeping up with my pace. Across the sky, the big ones collide and release flaming sparks, like firecrackers, loud.

Step inside, head for the grey door. Windows of the red house are painted white. Red house is carved of squares of sandstone. Yard is quiet but I can hear snoring and whispering and grunting and screaming from inside. Enter the house. Doors of rooms are white and numbered. The inside of the house itself is stony, unpainted and chilly. Floor is made of glass. Beneath it are empty rooms.

Stammerer tells me to remain at the door, near the crackling record player. She walks straight ahead. Disappears into the further darkness of the passage.

Wall is plastered with pictures. Images of naked women and men and a host of images I find grotesque. One is of a giant pressing his thick dick into a donkey's anus. Below it, another image shows a man who's about to cut the throat of a black goat while his accomplice cuts the balls off this beast. Black goat stares back at me. Wants to jump out of the image, embrace me, lick my dry skin and then beg me to prevent this butchery. Eyes are filled with life. Unsure if the people in these rooms know that the goat is alive in this image. Both frightening and fantastic.

Another image shows a man shoving a peeled banana into a woman's vagina while a black cow shits and urinates into her mouth as she lies sprawled under this animal. Her mouth is open wide, screaming, and the fountain of green soup from the cow's nether region is suspended in the air, on its way down into her gaping mouth.

Screaming and grunting from the rooms nearby keep punctuating my nervous breathing pattern. Confused. Is this place a brothel or butchery?

Remember grandmother's brother. Dubule. Grandmother told me about him. He was a shepherd. When he was in trouble, he'd rub his Rhino horn, sing a song and the song would deliver him by making him vanish.

In a dream, I didn't know where I was coming from. At the gate, I saw grandmother, mother, Dubule, aunt and little brothers gathered around our Datsun. All covered in colourful cloths. Only their snouts were visible.

Inside the car boot, a black coffin.

Stood among them. Instantly wrapped in a black cloth. They scattered, muttering meaningless phrases. Dubule dropped my corpse in the wheelbarrow and drove it away.

Hum Dubule's song, hoping it will distract me from the sad thinking. Sing the words of the song. Words don't leave my mouth in isiXhosa. Instead, they come out in English:

Dubule, Dubule
Cows of my father, Dubule
Let us go now, Dubule
We will be eaten, Dubule
By the grim

Decide to stop worsening my headache about the matter. Might be shaken by this strange place and people. Think of the bag of dagga I buried in a hole under my bedding and I sommer smaak to smoke. Must have been eza mpundulu that have stolen ubumdaka bam. Head throbs harder, my heartbeat quickens. Feel fear moulding itself into a boulder. Mounts my chest. Makes my breathing difficult. Insides of my nostrils are brittle and dry. Feel as though they would crumble and turn to dust if I were to sneeze.

Stammerer returns, followed by a man whose face structure and gait is familiar. Wait for the two to come closer to the light in the centre of the house. They finally reach me. Surprised to see Mthimkhulu here with the Stammerer. He is wearing a black dashiki and leather loincloth and sandals. His long tail jiggles like a starved serpent. Tail rubs his nose as though warding o' itchiness. He is not excited to see my face, looks irritated by my presence.

Feeling relieved, I shout, Ek sê Mthimkhulu! Words that slip out are, Big Tree!

Yho! I say. Word that jumps out is, Damn!

Can't control my tongue. A gap between my mind and my tongue. It has grown its own mind this very moment. Tongue refuses to say any of my thoughts in any language except English.

Shake my head and look again at the wall. Press and rub my eyes with my palms, and take another good look at the images. They have changed. Nothing is the same anymore. Images and drawings of dead musicians of all genres. Shake my head, thinking about the black goat, and say nothing.

Last night, I saw this black goat. Caught it tearing and eating at something rubbery with its teeth. This happened behind ibhuma. When the black goat saw me approaching it dragged its feast with its teeth, jumped through the bushes and disappeared into the night. Listened to my heart and did not go after it into that cold winter night. Know it is the same black goat, with teeth and claws like a lion's. It has the same necklace with a glowing dark blue stone around its neck.

Rush to Mthimkhulu, arms widespread. Want to bury my face in his chest, but he pushes me off, strikes me with the side of his right hand. Snort out blood, fall flat on the glass floor, marking it with trickles.

You, you, you have no, uh, he says, grappling for words, no respect!

Mthimkhulu grabs Stammerer's hands, says something in another language. He laughs. His voice is harsher than the usual voice he spoke to me with at umojiso. High-pitched cries roar out of the rooms. He twists his face and mouth when I look at him.

Hairy hand of Mthimkhulu holds my legs together, like iinkuni, and drags me along the dark passage way. Cries dissipate as he drags me further down the passage.

Scrape, cut my face. Trickles of blood trail along. He talks with great energy in another language. Punctuates his tirade by chewing stems of bushman's tea and spitting out a tiny ball.

Come to an unpainted, unnumbered room. He snaps his fingers. Door opens and the hairy hand throws me into the dark. Closes and locks. Surprised by the way Mthimkhulu is treating me here. Or maybe it's not him. I've heard of stories of people's lookalikes. Could be a lookalike of Mthimkhulu. But, if it is Mthi, how can he treat me like this, when I used to allow him to eat from ibhekile yam (ngecephe lam!), and did not mind him calling me by name, yet yityhagi?

Feel awfully cold, like am in a freezer. It's too dark to check if there's a bed or bedding in here. Fear moving about kanti there's a dangerous creature lurking in the dark. Stay still in this corner. After a while, I shout, Is someone living here? There's rustling. Funny noises and flashes of light come from the corner on my left. I just want something to cover my body. Lean against the wall. Wait for something to come closer to where I stand. Nothing comes, although the funny noises, flashes of light and rustling continue.

Slump ngeempundu with my back against the wall. Finger the Rhino horn. Sneeze from the stuffiness of the room. Rats crawl towards me. They playfully nibble at my feet. Some brush their hard heads against my hurting heels. Swat them away. They come back in a large group, making funny noises. Their eyes light up this part of the corner. They mount my feet. One big-headed rat stands on its hind legs on my knee, waving its tiny fingers at me. It jumps up and down thrice, sits ngeempundu. Rats are not really here to bite me to death as I initially thought.

They all gather, surround me. And then they begin running around, still making funny noises, nibbling playfully at each other's tails. Some tangle tails, organise themselves into a foot. The others form a right foot. Then, a stomach, a chest, arms, shoulders, neck and, finally, the head. Rat-human is marked with delicate blue lights. Can't say am shocked. Stand up and this rathuman is taller than I am. Looks at me and forms a smile. Then, after a moment, the creature squeaks. Points to the wall. Look up and see sloppy writing. Each time it squeaks, a tail writes sloppily on the wall.

The wall says: *We are Bed.*

Think for a moment. Then, I say, *OK*. The figure dismantles – rats spring to the floor and stand on their hind legs lighting their eyes on me. Half the rats crawl, form a figure on the floor.

The wall says: *Lie down.*

Place myself carefully on the backs of the rats, with my face looking at the roof.

Sleep on your stomach, says the wall.

Turn over. Umthondo slides into the mouth of the big-headed rat. Then, the other rats come on top, cover me with their woolly bodies. Surprised at the strength of these rats under my weight. Big-headed rat, whose mouth keeps umthondo, tickles my head with its tongue. It allows the tip to touch its palate. It licks, sucks it. Pleasantness of warmth massages me to sleep.

Another dreamless yet warm night passes. Sleep as though am in ibhuma. It's like the rat-human knows when I want to stretch my arms or legs, or switch sleeping positions.

Rats scatter, slip into the different holes in the corners of the room. Assume they are allergic to the sunlight that streams through the small window. Sit, leaning my back against the wall. Door opens. Mthimkhulu enters, holding a platter of grilled fish, two yellow buns and a bottle of red beer. Places the platter down.

Stands at the door, looks at me, says: *Eat.*

Swig the beer. Tastes like umdoko but is so bad it irritates my throat. Drink some more of it til there's little left. Don't want to o'end him. My body is still pained.

Fish has a putrid smell. Take bits of it and put it down. Chow the first bun, then the second one. Down the remainder of the beer. Makes me miss drinking umdoko nomqombothi.

You don't like fish, ey?

He gives me a shocked stare. Shake my head, say: Am allergic to fish. Not here, says Mthi.

He grabs my shoulders, lifts my tiny body ngedonga. You eat what we give, eh? You'll be a prisoner soon. Hahahahahahahahyoufuckenfoolhahahahaha!

He drops me down. This does not shock me. It hurts me. Think about it. In two weeks' time the elders are supposed to fetch me from Kwafindoda. Think of my big brother who's being trampled and kicked out emisebenzini nasemigidini because ijwabi lakhe was not cut in Kwafindoda or in Sakkiesdorp. Regain some energy. Mthimkhulu pushes my back, kicks me up the passage. Pass the rooms. High-pitched screams begin all over again. Heart pounds harder and faster. Stumble out the red house. Limp to the gate. Dreadlocked woman pulls one of her locs, the gate opens. He nods to her and says that he's taking me to the Black Hill of Bhakubha.

Take the left footpath that winds up. Runs along a

trench filled with black water. People on the side road
stare at me. Naked and my balls are bloated. Umthondo
has grown thick and long – Naliti was right about the
magic of ityeba! Kids point their short fingers and laugh.
They continue playing, still laughing, and tempted to
follow us. Women and men peer through the greasy
windows of their blue huts. Eyes analyse my existence.
Feel attacked by all these curious stares. Mthimkhulu
lookalike walks behind me speaking in another
language.

Pass white cows and black sheep grazing in the black
corn fields. They are thin and bloodless. Stop grazing.
Turn their heads to look at us. Follow us. Laughing kids
and old women and men join the group, with the lookalike leading them. Feel fearful and uptight. My body
twitches and my eyes itch with discomfort. Drag my
heavy feet and my big toe hits against a big yellow stone.
Thumps with a sting that makes me want to scream, sit
down and sob. Can't do that. Feel trapped like a crab
stuck between stones. Tears trundle down from my left
eye, monkey-like, but I quickly wipe them o' before they
see a Man crying.

Behind me, the mob sings. Melody of the song is
familiar but iyandidika this thing of not remembering
the words. Feel tired and confused. Walk wobbly up the
road. Red sun beats down hard. Bright redness of the
road affects my eyes badly. Stop for a moment and bend
over a puddle of muddy waters. See my gloomy reflection though the waters are dirty. My face has swollen
horribly, my lips are dry and my eyes are red with pain.
Umthondo lolls between my legs, stings each moment it
bumps against the insides of my thighs.

Walk a few more miles; arrive at the Black Hill of
Bhakubha. People are gathering around in a circle,

forming a courtyard. There's an opening before me. Step inside. The mob behind me closes the gap. The Witch sits on a throne of snakes. She is wearing a crown made of striking python- like skin. It shines. Flanking her are two irresistibly fine- looking women. Skin is bronze. Like the Witch, they are wearing beaded bangles, iinkciyo, naked from the waist up. Breasts are huge. Nipples touch their navels. Their red locs have made a mat on which the three Grootslange are coiled. Asleep. Shudder in fear for my life among these people.

People sing a song in unison. All their voices are soprano. Behind the throne of the Witch, hangs a line of big black mirrors. All of them are facing the red sun. Behind them, a woman holding ropes wheels the mirrors' movements. It's like she's controlling the light of the sun, but I don't know how she does it. She swings the ropes left, the mirrors slide right. Sun dims. Swings right. Sun beats down hard. Spins the ropes. Sun disappears. Holds the ropes tight and still. Sun reappears and dances. Goes on like this til the end of the song. She lets go of the ropes.

Everyone sits down on stumps. Remain standing, stunned at the three beauties before me. Snake in the middle, coiled in a heap in front of the Witch, loosens its body. Opens its big eyes and stares at me. Stare back and notice that the three women have not been moving their thick bodies. They are probably deaf with their dead eyes. Snake whistles and all the men amongst the children and women gather around me. Am in a pit standing on a red brick before the Witch and her three Grootslange.

Men begin urinating into the pit. Crowd jeers and screams. Snake wiggles its body in the sky, spitting venom. All their stinking urine reaches my knees. They walk back to the crowd, dabbing their dicks. Snake coils itself back and falls asleep.

One snake on the left opens its eyes and whistles. Flicks its tongue and spits out a hiss. All the dead-eyed children – boy and girls – piss for a long time. Urine reaches my waist. Snake falls asleep.

Snake on the right bends itself into a question mark its eyes still closed. All the women among the men and children gather around me. Squat and shoot out strong streams of piss. Hot piss lashes my face. Cracks of laughter spring from the crowd like bombs. Piss reaches my neck. Women all walk back to the crowd. Courtyard falls silent. Stinking smell of the piss chokes me, causes shortness of breath. Saltiness burns isinyenye, the calluses and scars on my body.

The Witch stands up. She moves towards me gracefully. Her eyes look really dead. They do not blink.

She raises her right hand, says, Red house, Bright house or Grey house?

Crowd jeers, shouts, Bright house!

She raises her left hand, the crowd quietens.

She says, Room of bodies, Room of mirrors or Room of stones?

Crowd jeers again, shouts, Room of bodies!

Something doorlike opens. Piss drains away in a noisy rush. Notice three openings that were not there earlier. Strong, sucking wind pulls me towards the opening on the right. Slide through the opening, hi!ing my head, elbows, knees painfully against its narrow walls. Glide down for a long time, hearing peals of laughter, jeering as though the crowd is still watching me down this hole.

Land ngeempundu in a very bright room with no doors, no windows. Brightness blinds my vision.

Squint. Walls are white; the roof is stark black. Hole in the roof closes completely.

Against the wall, kukho imizimba, standing before agape coffins, unblinkingly staring at me. Long nails have been driven into the tops of their heads. Sharp tips of the nails hang between their swollen thighs like short penises.

Stand up and examine the first one, on the right. It is Nomzamo, a woman from my township, who disappeared. It was in the seventh month that her scarred, bloated body was found at the mouth of some river in Uitenhage. My trembling fingers touch her purple face. Always wanted to fuck her. Her skin is shivering, frigid. Eyes are pale and, in her mouth, sharp piranha-teeth. Put my pinkie in her mouth. Her lips foam, gritting teeth grip, peel o' my fingernail. Blood spurts. Painful. Scream, only to be met with bombs of crazy laughter tumbling from the black roof. Look around, nervous. Brightness and imizimba rouses horror and confusion. Feel trapped, my temperature rises. Dampness clothes me.

Imizimba begin to tremble, dripping discharge from their mouths, nostrils. A noise, like someone drilling into something rocky, begins imitating the rhythm of their trembling. Trembling and drilling are one. Then, as if somebody has slung me, I glide violently towards the right wall. Hit my head hard against it. Blood showers out my mouth. Slip back towards the left, straining my elbow, hurting my back. It's as though someone has dropped, locked me in a matchbox. Now he has begun shaking it. But the coffins and imizimba are not moving. The shaking dizzies me, upsetting my stomach. I fart. Kak sprays out, draws the face of Phung' Amanzi on the floor. Flinch back in horror. The laugher restarts, sounding more sinister, sarcastic than before.

I cry out, What do you want?

The laugher stops. What did I tell you boy? Gruff voice of Phung' Amanzi. He started visiting me right after we buried Mandy, his daughter, my girlfriend, who died in labour. On his first visit, he told me, in a long trancelike tirade, that he was going to get me. Wanted to tell Father or Naliti about his threats. But he swore I would be struck dumb and lame if I told someone about his visitations.

He visits me during the day, riding his donkey- kaar, accompanied by his two deaf, dumb little girls who are always picking their noses with their toes.

At night he comes alone, riding his smoking pipe. Does not matter if am asleep. He enters my head and leaves me cold and wet.

Oh you remember now, boy! His threatening voice strikes back.

Breathe haltingly.

His laughing face appears outlined on the wall. In black paint. Room dims. Imizimba laugh, faces excited, I notice that most of them are my friends. One is Bu! Spencer. He's still burly and shaven, exactly the way he looked the day he died, in March, three years ago. He points at me, mumbles, his teeth cha!er. I froth with terror, the boulder in my chest jumps up. It replaces the ball in my throat. My throat and chest pain when I remember that I never went to his funeral. I cough, rack the back of my throat. It burns, I shudder, umthondo sti'ens.

The other one, Tero, straddles my chest. His wound is still bleeding. It was Maya who slashed his throat for failing to locate her clit with his tongue. He makes this mhmm- mhmm- mhmm sound edikayo and bullets of blood hit my face. His body is so heavy he could bulldoze me flat. He strikes me, and, when blood sprays out, he licks my nose with his lips, dripping mucus, saliva on my snout. He stops licking, and then, looks at me, eyes flattened as though he recognises my facial features.

Cry out, Tero?

He shakes his head, drives his long ring finger into my mouth. Finger nail scrapes the inside wall of the slim part between my eyes. My eyes redden numbly. Choke, cough, and vomit as soon as he takes his long-nailed finger out. He smiles, teeth haphazardly set apart.

Imizimba close their coffins, gather at the corner. They seem to be talking among themselves, but I hear nothing. Sit tired, numbed in the middle. Brightness vexes my vision.

Cuts on the inside of my throat. They itch. Imizimba, I think, communicate in sign language. They don't have tongues or iincakancaka. They make a noisy mhmm-mhmm-mhmm staccato sound, like my Mother, that conniving witch. It's because of her and that bastard, Father, that am stuck in this situation. They sent me to Kwafindoda. Wanted me to die. They are upset that their favourite son never had umgidi woqobo. Should have followed him, my big brother. This being a Man business is bullshit.

When I escape this place I won't even wait for the elders to come fetch me. I'll run into the township naked, find my big brother, tell him he was right about everything! Imizimba sit down in a circle and tangle their legs.

They are quiet, composed, as though sleeping, but I

doubt they ever sleep. Study their stillness. Pale figures, made of grit.

Think of Father. Heknowsaboutwhatishappening. A week before I was taken to esikhwetheni, Naliti told me that things were going to happen and he wouldn't be able to do anything to help me.

Father shouted, Uthetha ububhanxa Naliti, ucimba le ntwana inentaka?

Mother was sewing on the rocking chair; too deaf and engrossed in the details of her deed to fucking interfere. Remember the feeling that consumed me: numbness, similar to now, watching imizimba, and thinking of my doom.

On the wall, near imizimba, a dark door opens. A shadow jumps in, arms laden with iibhekile ezimbini. Flinch. Lean against the wall. Imizimba break the tangle, stand up, and make guttural noises. The shadow places iibhekile near imizimba.

Another shadow jumps in, carrying a big calabash. Imizimba take a few steps back to allow space for it. They kneel, bending over what appears to be iintsipho. They feed noisily, reminding me of a moment emojisweni when amanqalathi squatted around a big tub of boiled blood. They licked the tub clean and, on top of that, stick-fought over a huge chunk of meat. Miss the smell of roasting meat. Can't imagine any kind of meat. I have forgo!en what meat looks or tastes like. Looking at iintsipho, I think of the bad beer and foul fish I consumed earlier and feel nauseous, disgusted.

Though the room is still, each slurping sound imizimba make is an ear-splitting drill into my skull. The two shadows leave the room. Stare at umthondo. Feel a prickling sensation at the tip and around isinyenye. Bloated – isinyenye siyalila. Intlava has shrunk into a little moon. Shrinking by the minute. Imizimba stand up. Tero, Nomzamo and Bu! Spencer limp towards me, carrying the tub, while Laane's arms are laden with iibhekile ezimbini. My intestines twist into a fist. Taste a sudden rustiness in my mouth. The dark door opens. Phung' Amanzi jumps in carrying a nail as long as he is. He looks fresh and healthy. Nobody would mistake him for a ninety- five-year-old. He clicks in a perplexing language, shows no signs that he knows me. Somehow his indifference blasts my heart.

Tero twists and ties my hands behind my back. Gasp, bloating my chest. Butt Spencer keeps choking me with his right hand, deflating me. Blood jets out my nostrils. Phung' Amanzi laughs, pricking the tip of umthondo with the sharp nail. Stings horribly. Scream. Imizimba join me in the screaming. Scream for a long time til my voice turns hoarse, sounding like a crippled horn. Cough. Chest aches from the strain.

Butt Spencer chokes me once more. My voice completely dies. He snatches the necklace o' my neck. Shoves it in his mouth. Chews for a while, belches a gust of black smoke. I sneeze. Bu! Spencer keeps choking me.

Phung' Amanzi places the long nail on the floor. He grabs ibhekile filled with iintsipho. He commands Laane to squeeze my stomach. Tight. Tero kneels down, hugs my stomach with his dry arms, squeezing. Tight. Breathing is hard. My breath falters halts only to start once again. It's as if someone is squeezing breath out of my body only to blow it back in. Through my nostrils.

Phung' Amanzi opens my mouth roughly, cups iintsipho, stu' them into my mouth. Choke, he stu's, I choke, he stu's, I choke, coughing out bits of human nails. He stops. My head, chest, nostrils are heated. My eyes feel like they will blast out any moment I blink.

Don't know what am thinking. In my head an image keeps blinking, so fast I can't capture it.

Butt Spencer's hand chokes my throat, the image flashes away. My body aches. Can't breathe or relax. Tero holds me tightly, squeezing up a ball of kak that is not there. Butt Spencer is helping him to choke it up my gullet and get it out through my mouth.

Umchamo tinged with blood jets out. Hot stream aches. No control over my bladder. Laane squeezes, my stomach boils. Breath hurtles in gusts. Belch and fart. Stomach is empty as though amathumbu angaphuma ngeempundu if ndinosuza kakhulu.

Laane loosens his grip after Phung' Amanzi tells him to do so.

Nomzamo together with eminye imizimba, are watching, churning out the distant, dull, mhmm- mhmm- mhmm staccato song.

Tero unties my hands, pushes me hard. Fall flat on my face.

Someone drags me out of the room. A chill slashes through me. Outside. Isinyenye feels like ijwabi has just been sliced. Open my eyes slightly. It's night. Mob stands still around me, not even the trees dare quiver their branches. Everybody is naked. Can't identify the person who has dragged me back into this pit.

Everyone is singing the staccato song. Hyenas and the lions and the jackals and the trees have joined the singing. Next to the throne of the Witch, a smoking fire-place, houses imbiza yesiXhosa. Size of the three-legged pot says it can feed Bhakubha for three consecutive weeks. Pot is transparent. A tall creature drags his feet towards the pot. Can't see the person's face, it's dark, distant. Though my vision is vague, it's obvious that the person is a man. He's bare. Short penis stands still, almost buried under his bloated belly. He's carrying a tub. He puts it next to a square container. Heaves the tub, empties it into the pot. Tongues, iincakancaka, eye-balls, ears, fingers, toes, chopped penises swim in the boiling liquid. He lifts the container, empties the blood into the pot. Pot boils, like soup. Concoction thickens. In my stomach, the dizzying void widens.

Begins to drizzle in greyish streaks. Opposite the fireplace stands a bed of mud. It reminds me of Nomali. That's what she said at the funeral of Mandy. She looked me straight in my crooked eyes, said: Uy' ebhedini yodaka njandini! Her voice sounded sad.

We buried Mandy. Nomali's business plummeted. Mother's baritone voices creamed: Safayintakatho!

Afterwards Mother appeared deafened, dead to everything in our household, and especially in my life. Father looked at me for a long time, shook his head, bustled out the house. That's when he stopped smoking his pipe. He said it was about time he commits his life to the Lord.

I used to dream of Nomali. Dreamed I was stuck in a small cabin crowded by her countless apparitions, laughing, asphyxiating me. Could not tell Father. He believes abakhwetha are not supposed to see, think, dream of women.

Cold rain lashes against my bare body, punishing me for Father's foolishness. My body, a stone, hard, cold, almost freezes in this pit. Am the only one who suffers the cold drizzle. Here, everyone else is unresponsive to the weather. My mouth is wide open. Droplets contest in the wind. Each one wants to be the first to dive in to touch my tongue. Have not watered my mouth in a very long time. Rain water tastes horribly salty. Close my mouth, look around. Completely quiet now. Everyone is staring at the throne. Nothing is happening – the snakes, still asleep, and the Witch and her handmaidens, remain unmoved.

Above the throne, the sky is speckled with red stars. Rain only falls on the multitude and me. Find the discrimination disgusting. Don't want to annoy anyone here. Just want to find out why they are keeping me here when the elders and Ngaka will be fetching me soon. Or maybe this is one last test before I leave Kwafindoda. Truth is there have not been umgidi woqobo in my townships since Somagwaza. That was five hundred years ago.

Parents refuse to send boys to Kwafindoda. They say it is a haven for witches and wicked spirits. Boys go to Zanempilo Clinic, others to the bush in Sakkiesdorp. Boys that go to the bush in Sakkiesdorp say they are better off, more 'man' than Zanempilo clinic-men. All the drunkards of the townships attend imigidi of Sakkiesdorp men to drink umqombothi neqhilika . Nobody attends imigidi of Zanempilo men. No alcohol or traditional beers or stick fi ghting emigidini yabo.

Sakkiesdorp men and Zanempilo men axe and stab and shoot each other. Streets of our townships are wet with their blood and tears. The only proper Man in the townships who would be honoured with umgidi woqobo is any boy that buries ijwabi in the soil of Kwafindoda and returns home a Man. Father told me to become that Man.

———

Oohili come out of the bulrushes. Surround the throne, like short scruffy dogs, standing on their hinds. Astonished that they look different, their appearances not

even close to the grotesque creatures my Father is fond
of reading about in *Daily Sun*. Always hated them. Father
has a room in which all the issues of *Daily Sun* that talk
about them are kept. Images of ugly, black dolls are plastered on the black wall.

As a child, I once sneaked into the room. Father had
forgotten to lock it. Think he was stressed about my
sickly Mother. Studied the room and saw many portions
of flattened dough. Some stuffed with plastic eyes
gouged from the dolls. Other portions stuffed with
marbles for eyes. Those ugly dolls were frequent villains
in my nightmares.

Oohili turn around; face the throne, their woolly
backs dotted with big eyes. All the eyes dissect me,
weighing the very worth of my timid soul. Stare at the
lot of them til my eyes wet, head gets dizzy. Stare is stag-
nant. Seem to be staring into empty space – no throne,
no snakes, no Witch, no handmaidens, no starry sky, just
an expansive white blanket with blinking black dots.
Catch the sound of their every blink. Sound of a shutter
closing, the sound of umkhonto cutting ijwabi. Their
heaviness puts me in a trancelike state.

Do not even feel the lashing drizzle anymore, it's like
my flesh has gotten numb, or has become part of the pit
am in. Find it odd that I focus on petty things, not on
what is going to happen to me. Think a lot about grandmother, her sudden death. It was just a day after the
funeral of Mandy. She cried that a pair of sharp teeth
was moving up and down her leg, like a zipper. It
zigzagged, paralysed her entire lower body before it
went into her head. She was delirious. The nurses,
doctors at Zanempilo Clinic could not help her. Her big
toe ballooned, formed itself into a head with two ears
and a mouth. It said that grandmother is a witch who

hides her wickedness behind her church uniform. That grandmother should tell the truth, that she would sacrifice a member of the family.

Father and Mother suggested we suffocate the creature and grandmother agreed. We all knew the thing was ibekelo that was meant for me, but nobody said anything, the truth sat sadly in our heads. She had stepped on it during the funeral. In a dream she said things. It was a week after we buried her. She said to me things are going to happen but I should not be afraid, what will happen is natural. Hate to think she meant that am going to be another failed Man. It will break my Father. Mother is already broken, and appears half-dead, like a person who's alive only to grieve her slow, certain death.

Phung' Amanzi and Nomali arrive, riding imit-shayelo. They hover over the throne for a moment before they drop down and stand before the line of oohili. Hear nothing. Then, after a well-considered silence, the staccato song erupts. This time it is not coming from the multitude. It's also not coming from oohili. They don't look like they are very fond of song. Look around and can't see anything, yet the song keeps getting louder, more tedious by the second. It strikes me that the singing comes from the Bright house underneath me, through the openings on the corners. Phung' Amanzi and Nomali limp towards me, gripping imit-shayelo, like weapons.

Looking at me, they wrench their faces in disgust. Gather energy, shout, What did I do to you?

Nomali twists her mouth, spits at me, says: Who's paying my bills, uh?

Phung' Amanzi laughs, says: What did you do? You did not listen.

A piercing pain slices through my flesh. It's like all my pores are being needled. Like someone keeps prodding the needles to worsen the stinging hurt.

Shivering and fright take over my body.

Mouth shouts, Forgive me father. I must go home!

Phung' Amanzi chuckles and looks at Nomali.

Nomali stares at me, shouts, And you call yourself a Man?!

By now the singing has stopped. My heartbeat runs at an odd rate.

Tears well in my eyes. Can't hold them back. They roll down my cheeks.

Out of irritation, Nomali says: I said kill the thing and save my daughter. What did you say, eh?

Don't know how to answer Nomali. She looks exactly like Mandy, and this always confuses, frustrates me. Even in my dreams, I cannot tell between Mandy and her mother. Her face structure conjures Mandy into

memory. At the back of my mind, I see myself and Mandy playing, like the spectral figures of Lesilo and Vera, in a shadow show.

Nomali continues: You told your stupid mother about the pregnancy. Why, eh? Father? What did he name the child again, mhmm?

Phung' Amanzi spins umtshayelo wakhe. Grins and giggles. Oohili cackle, mouths crocodilelike. Cackle echoes and disappears in the depths of the bush. Comes back hard and bounces up. Flings back to blast my ears and grate my nerves with its chattering teeth.

Phung' Amanzi prods me with umtshayelo, says: It's a stupid name…I don't remember it now.

He always hated me, wanted Mandy to be with James Mfundo, the journalist, who publishes beautiful things about Nomali's iBheya business. But Mandy had always been mad about me. That they cannot change.

Doubt this place is under Perseverance River. Can't be true. Grandmother was a river-woman and told tales about the adventures she had undergone when she answered her calling. There was no mention of such wickedness in her tales. The waters must have gotten filthy over the years. People do all kinds of appalling things around the waters, especially at night, when they think no one is watching. They have sex and urinate and even crap near the water.

The other night, on my way to look for Mthimkhulu, I saw a bakkie dumping rubbish in the waters. Four white guys were brandishing guns about while two black guys were cleaning up the back of the bakkie and dirtying the waters. Hid behind a bush and watched them. Felt sad I could not do anything about their filthy job.

Begin to believe that this place is part of Kwafindoda. Density and darkness of the bush here is frightening. Eyes hardly penetrate beyond the front trees. They are close-knit, pressed, bound together, leaving little or no space for a mosquito to fly through. Visitors have to drop from the sky. No way I can escape this place if I choose to run away. Trees stand like guards, watchful of runaways. My hope for loopholes dies. Think of begging, but find no honour in such a shameful act. A Man does not beg, a Man endures to death.

Bring him here, commands Phung' Amanzi. Oohili jump into the pit. They are ten in number. They grab my arms, heave me, easily. Their short woolly arms rub softly against my bareness. Remain suspended in the air, supported by their huge heads. A bolt of silver light flashes between my eyes. So quick. So sharp. My eyes close, a black blankness. Head pains, when my eyes open wide.

Snuggled against the bed of mud, oohili surrounding me, predators. Each one of them clasps a knobby black stick. Phung' Amanzi, Nomali, Nomzamo, Bu! Spencer, Tero, Mthi and Laane are all here. There are many others whose faces I can't put names to. Facial features are familiar. I've met them before but don't know where, when, and this saddens and strains me. If I find something or someone to sympathise with my situation, I'll be better.

The Witch stands up. Everyone kneels down. Courtyard is quiet except for the intermittent croaking of cicadas, crickets, frogs from the nearest creek.

You two, the Witch points at Phung' Amanzi and Nomali, One more fieldworker or we take your daughter.

Her voice is horribly bassy. If she continues talking her words might rupture my eardrums. Mob mumbles and moves its heads about. Can't understand what is going on. The Witch whispers to her handmaidens. Grootslange wake up and wiggle. The Witch, handmaidens and the Grootslange vanish. Throne shrinks into a red dot which flattens into a black line, only to flash out of existence. Space is cleared. What is left is the imprisoning density and darkness of this bush. Everyone gets back on their feet. Hot waves from the fireplace brush my back warmly. Think of the concoction, wonder how long it takes to cook all the mess. Can't imagine myself eating human organs, sipping soupy blood for supper. But I'll do anything to go back to my township.

Oohili heave my body, place it on the bed of mud. Bed is hard, cold, sends shocking shivers down my back. See myself, like I've stepped outside myself, staring at oohili shifting, positioning my body, a prisoner, a patient on a stretcher. They rope my feet together. Hands too. Can't say anything. Voice has been eroded by fear. Looking at Nomali, I think of Mandy, something substantial in me breaks into bits of dust. Chest, throat is powdered in dust. How can they say I have killed you? Oh Mandy! Want to cry for her, but I can't, like that day at the funeral, my parched-eyes that burn like gas, cannot water. Wanted to hurtle my body into that pit, be buried with Mandy, my boy, inside the earth. That night, my big brother caught me carrying a pickaxe, a shovel, sleepwalking towards the graveyard.

Phung' Amanzi pampers my body with red powder. Nomali is helping him. Her hands touch only my upper body, it's Phung' Amanzi who treats my genitals. Badsmelling powder numbs me, putting me in a half-sleep state. Phung' Amanzi and Nomali are talking. Voices are distorted and distant. Everything moves sluggishly. At times, it's like nothing is moving at all. Think of the Red house, the many rooms that boomed with screams.

Think of the organs, the blood boiling in the pot. They belong to people I will never know, never meet. Or maybe they belong to the screamers. People I know, from my township, friends, who yelled like boys when they had to needle-and-thread off their dick-veins. No wonder they either went to Sakkiesdorp or Zanempilo. Think of the woman with long serpentine locs. Maybe her child's penis or tongue is also being cooked in this pot. Think of Mother. Of Father. Of brothers. Of Mandy. Of my dead- born boy. Of everybody I know. A slight vertigo creeps in, chokes me hard. Surges and swirls in me. Faces reel fast in my head. Ghastly image of my bloody boy does not banish from my mind. New images slide in. Flash through. Bloody, pain-tinged. Image of my boy sticks around in the shaded background, smirking.

An image: At the mouth of a river, standing on a jutting piece of earth, ready to drown myself. Sulking, the earth underneath me will crack and break soon. Image fades.

Bound on the bed of mud, again. Around me, dancing skeletons and scarecrows. Shot from the sky speeds towards my face. A nail aimed at my head. Never really reaches me. Bed of mud shivers, cracks. Sky is cracked. Clouds have been shattered, smashed in. They bleed pyrotechnics. Ears hurt from the drilling. Seems to roar from the sky, though the sky shows no signs of turbulent noise. Drilling blasts with a slicing pain, striking the middle of my head, so hard a vein bursts. It's like someone grips, uproots my hairs individually, violently. Black water shows me an image of Phung' Amanzi hammering a nail into a skull, hard. Every thud of his hammer hurts my head beyond endurance. No voice to shout, Stop!

Behind Phung' Amanzi, Nomali squats on the grass. She holds a sponge, snaps it with scissors. Bleeds, and my mouth froths. Drilling, the snipping, the stinging, halts my heart, for brief moments. Hiccup. Blood squirts. Gasp. Cough. Clots-shower out my nostrils ears mouths. Body convulses…things are smeared with vagueness, slipping into a deathlike stupor, being deafened, head-veins pound, ready to burst open, someone, something hacks my head hard.

HIGHWAY

Peep through the keyhole. Eyes cut through the concrete walls. In the next room, in front of the mirror the two deaf, dumb little girls in black dresses trim their long hairs. Blonde hairs so long they drape over their faces and hide their eyes. Nomali shakes their shoulders, shouts at them to make haste and not be late. Plop the iron haircombs on the floor, run out of the room swinging their suitcases, ignoring their mother's voice. In the kitchen, the four shepherds–Malahla, Nxilandini, Nkawu, and S'fombo – are sitting on a bench, each holding a litre of Mageu. Phung' Amanzi barks, walks up and down, stalling to go out.

He says: S'fombo, you fucking that stinking bitch of yours, don't guard my cattle, you think pussy will pay you, mhmm?!

S'fombo coughs, sips, and says nothing. They fear Phung' Amanzi's rough beating. Maya leans against the blue wall, folded-arms, dimpled-smile and gap-teeth. She's the only one whose face is gentle and composed. She grabs a broom, walks out the kitchen. My eyes follow her steps into the bedroom. Maya pushes the door open, enters, and brooms the carpet. She casts looks, but does not near this side of the room. She knows am in this wardrobe, she's just avoiding me. All the family members know about this beast locked inside this drawer. They are all indifferent.

Tried to step out. Was one of those dull days, when Maya was not around the house, humming while cleaning or cooking. I could not escape, I felt sick, stomach twisting and turning as though boiling dregs of beer. That time. Was frantic, not yet used to the dullness of the wardrobe. Crammed among a jumble of scarred shoes grubby socks stained panties bloody pads petticoats oversized bras black head wraps blonde wigs.

Eyes, hard, cannot wink. Muscles stiffen. Body heats up. In my left ear, Nomali snores, a pig. Something in this wardrobe that wards o' transgressive thoughts. Am bound, a caged beast, though my vision is not sheltered. There has to be another way around this annoying thing. Can't listen to her snoring, gossiping and shouting. Her panting during her fucking with Phung' Amanzi or Ntonga the horny hili is the worst. Shameful to allow such racket for the rest of my days. There has to be a way of turning off her grating voice in my ears. At least a switch – off during the day. Asleep or awake, her noise has no limit. Words coming out her mouth are becoming inseparable from my own thoughts.

Hours since Phung' Amanzi and his four shepherds left for ebuhlanti.

Almost evening now. Two girls return from school around this time. Odd how they have not. On the couch, Nomali talks in her sleep. Two voices: one snoring, another, talking.

Garbled sentences slip out her drooling lips: I did to

your son Nocwaka…beat you up, what is this, eh? Ubani? Mna? Did it to save my own daughter…. yes, yes, oh Mama, I tell you the truth… it's like that and no, it's not like this, oh please…who? I know what I am doing… for my daughters!

Don't know how to take this.

A recurring dream, since that week I arrived and lived in this drawer.

She blinks.

Her eyes are now watery, appearing shaken by shock.

She yawns, arising from the couch as though slipping out of a daze.

She yells, You will never harm me!

Furtive, she looks around, hurries into the bedroom.

Shoves her arm under the mattress, brings out a white handbag, places it on the bed, and culls out a smaller plastic bag.

Contains my bodily hairs – eyelashes, moustache, goatee, pubic and underarm hairs, even my toenails and ubumdaka bam.

She sprinkles a powder into the plastic bag, shouting, Heh wena! Kutheni la njakazi unyoko indinyela ngoku?

She burns a sprig of impepho in the middle of the room.

Oohili drop down into the fireplace. Mlambo slithers out from under the bed.

They all gather and encircle Nomali. Oohili clap hands and chant and dance Nomali into a silent trance.

Two deaf, dumb little girls arrive. Drop their suitcases at the door. One goes into the bathroom. Other one remains sitting in the lounge, on the couch, nestling a radio. She fiddles the knob. Screeches. Distorted noise fills and heats the house, breaks the light bulbs, cracks the windows. Insects buzzing and rubbing their tiny bodies against the windows shake and fall. Spoiled brat grins, rubbing her lips with her big toe. Look away from these sick selves. Pay attention to myself. Vision and hearing are sharp, I pick up every bit of information in the house. A recorder, my eyes and ears are constantly seeking something, anything, as long as it's within the margin of Nomali's house.

Phung' Amanzi enters the house, the bedroom, lights dim. Body loosens as the sky blackens and moonlight brightens. Wonder what will happen if, one evening Phung' Amanzi doesn't return. Spell lifts at the exact time he steps inside the house. Can't stand the thought of being trapped in this wardrobe at night. Who will help my mother Nomali do serious work for the Witch of Bhakubha? Can't be Bhogrom. Bhogrom can't do things with stealth, can't work without the heavy chain he trails noisily, inviting dogs and the curious living.

Last week he left us stranded in Sakkiesdorp. Nomali and me were inside the house, poisoning Nyathel' Igqwirha. He's the shebeen owner who is to blame for the collapse of Nomali's iBheya Garage. Glad he's dead. He swallowed a cupful of red ants and they ate his entrails in return. We tiptoed out his house and Bhogrom was chasing dogs in the street. Nomali became angered and began shouting curses. Lights inside the house flickered on. We panicked, hid behind an apple tree. Dogs howled from the street, feet thumped, voices susurrated, gun shots fired. Bhogrom did not think. We could have been killed had someone seen us naked in the yard of Nyathel' Igqwirha! Pulled out ikrali yam, pointed out that we should leave Bhogrom behind and ride ikrali back home.

Nomali walks in, unlocks and opens the wardrobe, slides the drawer open. She snaps fingers, says a long spell only the witches know and can recite off-by-heart, calling upon the name of Gqwirha Elimhlophe and the Almighty Mdalidiphu. Phung' Amanzi relaxes his legs and starts beating down the djembe with his feet while Ntonga the horny hili dances with Nomali. Spring to the carpet, straighten my arms and legs. Can't explain the feeling of being freed from being packed like a parcel in the drawer. Throw my legs and arms about trying hard to stay in line with the rhythm of the djembe and the chanting. Copy the movements of Ntonga, but Bhogrom dances better than me. He's on the windowsill, clapping his huge hands, jumping up and down, bobbing his head, showing his red gums, as though he thinks Nomali is going to send me to the bush. He has no idea I work in the township tonight.

Walk to the graveyard. Find Sporho curled into a foetal position against the headstone. Sporho and me play Tsi Gxada. It's his favourite game. We flurry to the Highway, me pale with ikota, Sporho dark-faced, his black jacket drooping over his bony shoulders. Our feet do not touch the road. Speed leaves a trail of shaken dust and gutted weeds circling in the atmosphere. Takes us exactly three heartbeats to get to the Highway. The dark bush overlooks the Highway, like the shadowy face of a giant ghost with bushy hair, opening its mouth to receive Highway motorists. Face of the ghost is a massive dark painting spreading across the starry sky.

Everybody can see this painting except the self-absorbed living. This is where Sporho died, though he never thinks to me the details of his death. But it does not matter, does not change the relations of our friendship. Can almost see that the Highway was not always this way. Something sombre must have happened to Sporho for the Highway to be frowned upon by his shadowy face, whose mouth is the gateway to death and decay.

Small cars and buses stream by as we stand on the side gravel road. Prefer delivery trucks. Three appear from edolweni, hissing gusts of thick breath. Pick out the last one. Jump in the passenger seat. Person is alone. Listening to the radio, Rock blaring. Truck carries six shipping containers. Hairy face opens his mouth and puts of grey smoke jet and dampen the rear-view mirror. He slides open a small drawer – an ashtray. Stubs the entjie, closes the drawer, takes out a tissue paper and wipes o' the mirror. One stroke. Hairy face sees me in the mirror, screams, horrorfilled. Swings and sways the truck.

I smile at him coldly as he loses control of the wheel. Pissing and shitting. My face in the mirror is swollen and dry with ikota. Sporho and me get out and watch as he crashes the speeding truck against a stream of oncoming cars. Truck swings askew, hurling the containers onto the road. They flip and roll over and smash all the cars nearby and behind. Cars speeding from behind crash their noses against the containers rolling on the road. Blobs of blood and screams shatter windscreens. A jumble of bones and bits of battered flesh and shattered windscreens and jagged broken teeth in a mixture of blood and tears and shit and petrol have written themselves on the road. This one badly-injured motorist nervously opens his car door. Hurls his body out onto the dead road. Crawls up trying to get on his knees. A shipping container flips, rolls over, smashes, squashes his flesh and bones to blotches of paste on the street.

Look at Sporho, he nods his head. His skeletal right hand points at the road ahead. I smile. I have swallowed my tongue. Sporho can't talk either. Our language is chaos, death. Meander the night. Our electric bodies buzz, rattle streetlamps, hound empty buildings, break windows, terrorise the living. Thread through dark, quiet streets, messing directions of midnight marauders, pedestrians. Not everyone sees Sporho. The living feel his turbulence. He flings, kicks objects, stones, empty cans, tables, chairs, droms, and trolleys to make his presence felt. Follow and freak out this old man.

He acts timid, looking back and sideways every second. Can smell his fear and panic. Stench irritates the insides of my hairy nostrils. The boulder thumps lousily against his tiny chest. He carries a Shoprite plastic bag, staggers up the dark street, reaches the mid bump where Sporho and me are standing, leaning against a Danger container. Flick out an entjie stub before his feet. Sporho flames it with his fingertips. Sparks like an ember. Instead of stamping it, the stupid man skips it. Sporho snatches and drops him in town. In the morning, pedestrians will find him hooked, straddling the huge wooden gate of the Methodist Church, dreaming he's riding a horse- woman.

My appearance freaks out the living. Must be disturbing to those who know me, seeing me roaming the streets, barefoot, pale. But such encounters are few. Am now barred from the east side of the township, where the living want to lure me into snares. My mother Nomali laughed bitterly, said: They will never get you mntwana wam!

It was last night. Stepped on a puddle, feet- stuck on

mud, and could not move my lower body. Nomali shouted at me, calling me all kinds of insults. She dropped next to me. Saw ibekelo, silently mixed a concoction, made it boomerang back to the owner.

We lifted o' the ground, ballooned back to Bhakubha.

Sporho and me soar to the west side of the township, our eyes fixed on network of streets as though looking for the owner. Taverns and shebeens are closing. Dark gravel streets blast the night with high-pitched yelping and barking dogs. We hover for a while, looking to land on a dimly lit street. On Government Avenue, lamps are all o'. All good for us; we cannot handle much light and a sea of drunks. Car boots are open, music booms. Iimpundu ezinkulu bounce up and down in white jeans like pairs of lightning bolts in the dark. Against the car, couples are having fun – hugging, kissing, groping, fondling each other's genitals. Horny-humans, all around. All they care about is noisy drinking and fucking. They don't respect the night, its oddities, its function.

Stand meters away, near a Danger box. Something about Danger containers that excites the energy of Sporho. Electricity supercharges his affection for terrifying and torturing the living. He becomes violent and unfeeling. Throws stones and pokes random people we come across as we travel through the streets of the township. That's not all. This one night, we followed a fat man, and Sporho suggested that we lead him to the train station. Sporho compelled him to sleep with his legs across the train tracks. Waited til the train appeared in the distance. Watched the train cut the man's legs, blood spattering, staining the windows. Man's cry was excruciating. Train was forced to come to a halt. Walked away, listening to the sweet sound of screams coming from inside the carriages. Smiled cos I don't feel anything for the living. Just want to hurt them. Sporho agrees with my thought. He thinks it's human foolishness that has cursed us to live this lonely life.

Woman comes. She squats, her back against the Danger. She sprays out a stormy fart and Sporho thinks it's disrespectful. Rub my eyes with my fists, chew the leaf of the zebrawood, spit in her face and spellbind her to unsee me. Not in the mood to deal with all the sick timidity of the living. When they see me or Sporho, they scream, they run, terrified. Others even get epileptic and die. What a joke! Before I met Sporho it was di'erent, I did not have any spells. Nomali would send me to some house to dig a hole and bury the cursed seeds of umthi kaMlanjeni. I'd always do it in fear of coming across a powerful person – igqirha okanye ixhwele under the guidance of Ngaka. Nomali does not want to give me spells.

Each night, she only gives me the seeds of umkhokha to pocket in my pouch, saying they are for protection. She says I want to manipulate her spells to escape the wardrobe. She thinks she's playing safe, but when she's asleep her lips slip out things that she should not be saying. That's how I snaffle most of her spells.

Woman pulls her jeans up, zips them up, and belts them. Look at Sporho. Can't say what he makes of this woman. He's quiet. Be!er for me if he's being nostalgic, it gives him more energy and hatred to go around playing Death. We set o' from the ground, drift towards the street the woman walks in. She pushes her body forward, hands flail, pulls it back and sways sideways, staggering, as though uqhuba amatakane.

Float above her head. Frantic, she turns back. Eyes pop out, skin, goosebumped – unamanwele. She rushes, trips, falls on her side, her left ear bursts open, blood streams. Like a wounded beast, she struggles to get on her feet. Can't keep the balance, can't stand, legs too lame. Falls, bruises her knees and elbows.

She crawls.

Sporho flings a torn shoe at her heels.

She belches, screams, Ndiyeke nja! Ndiyeke!

A dog runs out of some house, barks after her. It does not see us.

She stands up, drunkenly. Dog keeps barking but never reaches her legs to bite.

She sways towards a grey house, pushes the gate open, heads for the door.

She pounds the door with her fist and yells, Vuka! Vuka! Vula lo mnyango!

She stops. Silence. She panics, head rotates, hands quiver.

Lights turn on. A half-naked man unlocks, opens the door. She flashes inside.

He steps outside, stands on the stoep, barefoot, looks around briefly, walks back inside, closes, locks the door. Sporho looks at me. He wants to show me something.

Yard is light, ayiqiniswanga. When the lights go o' we walk into the house through the front wall. A four-roomed house: a lounge, kitchen, bedroom and bath-room. In the dark corner of the bedroom, I watch the woman undress. Her wide and thick hips tickle the tip of my nail and stiffen umthondo. Sporho would enjoy seeing her having ibhentse yakhe pricked ngesikhonkwane. Her mouth is foul. Even the dry breath that hurtles out her nostrils – the sound of it plopping on the floor – spreads a maddening smell.

Her hollow heart drums oddly against her hardened fistlike breast. In my ear the sound is of a fist banging on a wooden door. She winces from the cut on her ear. Dabs and presses the t-shirt against her ear, wraps the t-shirt around her head. She takes o' her panties, bra, slides into bed next to the man. Wait for them to fuck. But the man does not even make a move nor does the woman. An hour passes, nothing happens. Easy for me to hammer a nail into his penishole, or compel this woman to strangle this Eunuch. This happened with the other couple we followed. The woman drowned the fucker in the water they were fucking in. Half an hour later, we compelled her to hang both their bodies. On umsimbithi tree, a metre away from the mouth of the Perseverance River.

Compel the man and the woman to descend into deep sleep. Sporho slides to my corner. Hot air floods out his big nostrils. He touches the woman's head with his flaming fingertips. Her forehead heats up, ears redden, hair dampens. She sleeps with her big eyes open. Sporho smiles, touches my hand and turns me into a spirit. Jump into her eyes and enter her dreamscape. Place is a long empty dark street with a deafening silence. Not even a hum of wind. Just a vast blackness in front of me that spirals further into an endless sea of blackness. Do not see anybody. No animals, no sky, just beer bottles and entjie stubs here and there – a mind of a petty person.

―――――――

Wander, wallowing in the blackness, observing, but nothing strikes me.

In the back of my mind, the voices of Phung' Amanzi and Nomali, a grating noise obstructing me from focusing on my own thoughts.

Nomali: We have to take it out, we must. It is not working with us it must go.

Phung' Amanzi: It'll get what's coming to it.

Nomali: Who should we send for this? We don't want mistakes.

Phung' Amanzi: Send uSihamba Ngenyanga. Bhogrom will not do a very good job. We don't want to be caught in this…

Nomali: Dig a hole, spread the seeds, sprinkle the black powder and cov- er with earth. Wait for the black flower to grow, pluck its leaves, go inside his house, make sure he chews and swallows.

———

A thought hits me. Nod and think to Sporho the dream.

Woman is locked in a house. Eunuch has left for the shop down the street. Zim appears, walks to the house, carrying imbawula evuthayo. He puts it down next to the door, takes out the hot iron, and swallows. Burns his throat, softens his voice. Knocks on the strong door.

Who is it? shouts the Woman, frying meat in the kitchen, thinking it can't be the man.

It's me, open the door, says Zim.

It's windy, and she can't really tell if it's the man talking. She walks to the window, peers, but it's too dark to see the face. She sees the white shoes, the black trousers, but had not really noticed the clothes he wore on his way out.

Come to the window, show your face, says Woman. It begins to rain, very hard.

You want me to get wet? yells Zim after a well- considered silence.

Zim smiles, rubbing his hands together, his back bent under the canopy of the door.

Sing my favourite song, sing it now, urges Woman.

She quietens, puts her ear against the door. All she hears are raindrops hurtling against the roof like comets. She thinks it's unfair to ask the man to outsing this downpour. It really must be the man, she thinks. Maybe the Somali shop down the street is closed. She opens the door. Zim jumps in, chokes her neck with his huge hand. She screams. The deluge drowns her thin voice. He tears her nightie open with his nails. Baggy breasts burst out. She yells, kicks, punches. He answers her with a hard smack across her face – blood and spittle spray out. Licks the liquids. She shakes, humming her cry, punctuating it with hiccoughs. He takes out a knife-blade from his bag, sniggers, flashing his sharkteeth.

Zim holds and folds the Woman's locs into a bundle. Fastens, clinches them it into a !st. With one hand he lifts her body. She shrieks, kicks convulsively – more pleasure for Zim. He thrusts the knife-blade into her throat. Pushes it, twists – a screw. Drives it once more with great force. Knife-blade slips through, falls behind her. A bloody hole. She coughs out blood, wants to yell, but, instead, blood squirts out the hole. Zim shoves his tongue into it, licks, sucks, drains the blood. He removes his tongue, plunges his right hand into the hole. He pushes it deep down. Holds the heart, squeezes, uproots it, leaves the body to fall on its back. It's cold, bloodless, petri!ed. Woman turns into wood. From his bag, he culls a hatchet, begins chopping the wood into equal chunks.

Sporho touches the Eunuch's head. Skeletal fingers grip and drag me out of his dreamscape. A sleep soaked in blood and sweat. Sporho thinks it's going to be great news when the Eunuch wakes up in the morning to the mutilated Woman.

BLACK LEAF

J ump through the window. Blast down the dark street. Wind, the grumpy beast rages, digs, uproots weeds from between the pavements. Shakes and rips roofs off. Corrugated slices of sheeting from shacks speed to stick against the gaping gate of the graveyard. Along the road, Sporho flings objects at dogs we come across. This one here has broken its left foreleg. Yowls, drags its loose limb into a yard. House is situated opposite the crowded cemetery. Fence is halfway done.

Lights are off, shadows sprint to and fro in the yard, dancing to the wind, like demented dogs. Yard is heavy with ikhubalo. Already I see snares set in different parts, wires twisted into strange figures and leaves of grass bent in weird ways. Read symbols. Here, next to the gate, is a little beaded bottle roped around the pillar on my left above my head. This ikhubalo is meant to ward off oohili but it has lost its strong preventative power.

Above the white door of the house is the same bottle, but it's half empty. Can't quite tell what kind of ikhubalo it contains. Wounded dog squeals, trails blood and drags its leg into a kennel. A tall man attends it. Can't find soil – near this gate, it's all cement. My fist strikes the floor hard, cracks it open, earth appears. Slip the side of my hand into the fissure, grip, pull out the boulder. Maggots, earthworms, bugs, grubs twist, turn as though frying in a pan. Scoop a palmful, empty it into my mouth, down my throat. Fingers deepen the hole. Soil is moist. Gobble all insects on sight. Sporho hangs over me, a guardian. Tall man runs into the house. Dog looks in our direction, it's aware we are here. If we go any nearer, its eyeballs will explode with terror.

White, woolly seeds sleep in the rectangular hole. Empty the powder over them, cover it with soil. Squat, back against the pillar, waiting for the flower to sprout. Man returns, holding a purse and a plate. Study the actions of the man and the reactions of the hurt dog. Why does he think he cares so much for this useless thing with three limbs and slimy eyes?

Man is ridiculous, running around in this turbulent wind over the petty health of this fated animal. He pushes the plate near the head of the dog. Dog muzzles the plate away without even sniffing the food and goes back to squealing. Spoiled brat! Desire to slit the throat of this noisy dog with my metal nails grows stronger each moment I realise the flower has not grown. My mother Nomali did not say how long it would take for the flower to spring. Might as well go cut the dog's throat, scare the man and watch him run after his last breath. Man, not knowing what to do with the pain and tricks of his dog, hurries into the house. Bangs the door, lights go off. Knew he was going to get tired. Men are not patient with animals, with anything. Skin of the shadows thickens; they now stroll about the yard with an arrogant gait, arms splayed. Two in number. Watch them lurch towards the wincing dog. They kneel before it.

One of them, with the boldest arms and legs touches its swollen face. Eyes flatten and its body gets epileptic. There's no use for it to go through all this stupid suffering. Slitting its throat is the solution. But the shadow does not cut the dog's throat. Instead, he takes iintongo with his fingertips and smears their juice on his eyes. Hide, lest his plan works. Belief is that, when one smears on one's eyes iintongo of a dying dog, one achieves a heightened sense of vision, allowing one to see oohili, iziporho, izithunzela neempundulu. Not sure about being seen. Angers me that the shadow leaves the dog, dawdles towards the direction the dog's head is facing – towards me and Sporho. Hands twitch, not from the bad-tempered wind, but from the facial expressions of the forthcoming shadows.

Flower has grown. Leaves are thick, black, hard like the skin of black oranges that sprout only in the soil of Kwafindoda. Pluck them, leaving the flower a bare stick, tiny and sharp like a needle. Dig up the stick and slide it into my pouch. Take out my knife-blade, begin chopping, grinding the six leaves into fine powder. Organize it into a heap. Take the remaining leaf, place it inside my pouch. Bottle the powder. Dog is now either dead or unconscious. Can't hear its pulse or breath. Stand up, lurch towards the door of the house, trying hard to make as though I don't see the shadows. Take one more step past the third pillar. A hefty punch on the side of my head sends me floating on the grit of the earth. Hit my mouth against a sharp rock – painful – though my flesh is rubbery. Tall shadow with bold arms and legs stands over me, as though to say, Get up and fight.

Sporho struggles with the other one. Sporho is lucky;

he can vanish any moment he feels tired – go away to gain energy and reappear as he likes to resume the fight. Stand up, pull out ikrali and prepare to beat the shadow to death. But he is quick on his feet. One moment he's on the ground, the next move he crawls walls. He laughs as he ducks all my powerful stickstrikes. Strike once, jump back when I miss his black skin. Sidestepping my strikes, he manages to land several blows to my head. Grabs me, his right hand holding impundu yasekunene, left hand, gripping a mesh of my chest-flesh, throws me up. Spring up, trampoline-style. Arc up, a swift stone. Come down, crunching my head hard against the bark of the lucky-bean tree. Nail wobbles and my vision vagues. Thrash down ngeempundu.

Shadow stands on the stairs and waits for me to screw and tighten the nail. Hate fair people in fights. Hate his arrogance, as he waits and looks at me with his white eyes. Wish I had my panga with me to cut this bastard's black body into blocks of coal. Ikrali might break in half if I keep missing the shadow and flogging my stick against the earth or concrete. Hammer the head of the nail with my palm. Clicks back into its hole, restores my vision. Shadow vanishes, appears behind me. His huge hand sends me floating in the air. Come down thrashing against the kennel. Topples rolls over and sticks against a pillar. Dog is really dead now. Falls on the ground, a soaking wet rag, body heavy with blood. Shadow has disappeared. His fists are a big deal. Have not winced from dizziness in a while. Wish Bhogrom was here, to help me chain this bastard and beat him into a wreck!

Limp a few steps forward, hide in a dark corner, behind a dustbin. Here, in the back yard, it's silent. Take out the bottled powder, palm a bit of it and rub it on the skin of ikrali. Suddenly shines. Close the bottle and place it back into my leather pouch. Wait for the shadow to appear and ambush me, since he thrives in the darkest corners of the night. Ikrali feels much heavier now – powder-powered. Hearing is sharp enough to hear the tall man's snoring. Maybe it's the house that's heaving, through its concrete skin. It's like the house is shifting and drifting closer to point out my hiding place. Annoying and noisy. Shadow thinks he is tiptoeing, but his click-clacking footsteps are outrageously loud now – a 50 pound sledgehammer struck against a wall, again, an explosive sound of a bursting head of a body dropped from the 50th floor, then, each thumping footstep, a fired bullet.

Smell his distance. He's almost here. Hide my weapon behind my back. As soon as he appears behind the dust-bin, I pull out ikrali and stick it out, pointing at his direction. Works like a spell. Pulls him towards me, lame, helpless. Strike him between his eyes so hard – they pop out and float like two white marbles. Spin in the dust, muddying their white skin. Heel them and the black juice jets out and marks the white wall of the house. He batters against the grit of earth, spreads out on his back on the ground, a cowardly log. Grab him up, hold him in the air, and then crunch his burly body into the dustbin. Sick bastard! Almost got me.

Join Sporho to help him out, but he has already solved the shadow. Shrunken shadow is crammed in the corner of the yard, petrified, arms broken, limbs criss-crossed. Sporho smirks and we walk through the concrete wall. Astonished that the skin of the house has not resisted us or punched us out. Nyathel' Igqwirha's house's skin did. Grew these thick concrete arms on the sides and punched and jabbed me to the ground. Could not get inside. Hands held me to the ground. My mother Nomali had to travel all the way from Bhakubha to help me out.

TV is talking to itself or to the empty room. Go through the kitchen door. Smell of impepho hanging in the air tingles the insides of my nostrils. Sneeze for some time and then I hiccup. Floor is strewn with wooden crosses and open Bibles and specks of salt and red pepper. Don't know why people are stupid enough to believe that sprinkling red pepper and salt somehow repels oohili or a person like me. Still don't know how all of this is supposed to save anyone from anything.

Along the passageway, a door on the left is open. Step in. Kids' room, a boy and a girl, asleep. Room smells of stinking shoes and piss. Sporho stares at the black and white television ide iphum' estishini. Get out, leaving Sporho giving the kids nightmares, cursing their blue-eyed dolls and toy guns. Step in the next room, dim and slightly stuffy. Immediately. Sense something shifting. Not sure what it is. Might be the house. Once heard Nomali telling my father Phung' Amanzi about some house that locked its doors. She could not walk through its wall, it grew thick iron spikes. Drifted and went to puke her into the waters of Perseverance River. Her body crashed through the window. But she said she was lucky that she did not leave her broom outside. She straddled umtshayelo wakhe and flew away as soon as the house emptied out.

Front window of this house seems to have shifted – now faces the east. Door through which I entered faces the south. Confused as to whether to register this as an omen or just a trick the tall man is trying to play. He looks like he's in his forties, tucked in his double bed like a dead thing. Radio is playing loud music. His dombo and mdoko belly bulges behind his grey duvet. Stand watching from this black corner, staring at his horribly long legs and huge feet. His mouth is slightly open, drooling kota-white saliva. Dreaming, snoring. All better for me. Sprinkle the powder all over the room, around his face and rub it behind his ears and on his moustache. Powder dissolves into moisture, becomes his sweat.

Slip the leaf between his stinking lips. He does not chew the leaf, the scent of which is a mixture of lavender and mint. He holds it with his tongue only to push it out. Does this each time I slip in the leaf. Annoying. Wonder what will happen if I simply slit this man's throat instead of going through all this slow work of poisoning. But my mother Nomali said she does not want any mistake. Might as well do what she dictates. If only Mthimkhulu was here now, that cunning mbulu, he changes himself into any animal he fancies: hare or cow. Sure he'd think of a smart way to trick the man into chewing the leaf.

Take the leaf, tread to the kitchen. Inside the fridge there is nothing but drought in the form of a half-cut small onion and a bottle of lemon-cucumber water. What a pauper. His pots are almost empty. One has chicken gravy and two pieces of meat, the other one has a scoop of yellow rice. If tonight he ate this chicken and yellow rice, I might as well work with that. Have not yet succeeded in inventing a loophole, a backdoor entrance into his head. Look through the kitchen window and imagine the moonlit midnight endless, no imminent sunlight, no having to undergo the tedium of being stuck in a drawer with lifeless inert things. Next to the clock on the wall, an image: the tall man's frame draped in a black suit, next to him, a girl, his daughter, in a graduation outfit, brooding.

Walk back to his room. Sporho is giving him a hard

time. Man is sweating intensely, afflicted with convulsions like his epileptic dog. He's having a horrible dream, no doubt, but it's not the kind I want him to have. Can tell the man has been worked on, he's not an easy chap, and it's even hard to jump into his dreamscape. Can only watch and hope for the best. Transparent blanket boomerangs me back each time I hurl myself in. Each tic of the long hand of the wall clock is an axe hacked into the flesh of my nerves. All he dreams about is fucking little township bitches he picks at shebeens or taverns, takes home in exchange for a plate of chicken and yellow rice.

He trembles, his pajamas soaking wet. Pissed and shat in his pants. Man really wants to wake up but the medicine has sunk in his skin pores and keeps him locked in the same dream though the fucking is with a different bitch. Sporho disallows the man to break from this circle. He thinks it will crack a hole in the blanket, but it's the 25th time now and nothing has happened, except the man's bed has transformed into a pool from his sweat and piss. In his dream he cums, in bed he pees.

Take out the bare stick from my pouch and begin whipping the man's soles lightly. He winces, cheeks dimple, his eyes now slightly open, and his mouth froths. Ease, lighten up. Tighten my grip on the whip and hit him much harder than before. With another robust strike, his eyes open wide. White eggs. Take out the leaf, slip it into his mouth, with my right hand I shut his mouth closed. Leaf does not move afterwards, and the odd thing is that he has also stopped dreaming. His mind is now blank and his heart is not beating. This worries me. What if this is not what my mother Nomali wanted me to do with the tall man, what am I going to do if things don't go according to her plan?

Sporho notices that I have stopped bothering with the tall man's lifeless body, that am looking through the window, at all the sorcerers riding their brooms and baboons to Bhakubha. They all fly near the moon. Everybody can see this image, except the self-absorbed living engrossed with flea-scratching. Tall man's burly body is being cooled down by the pool in which it bathes. Sporho puts his hands around the head of the man. He manages to heat up the man's head, but he shows no signs of a thumping heart or twitching eyelids or moving mandibles.

Near his face, snap the mouth open. Position of the leaf remains unchanged, no new movement recorded. Makes me sick and deranged with nervousness. Grab the bare stick and start pounding his soles again. With an enormous force, channeled into my hand, strike the tall man. His eyes blink once. And snap closed. His mouth moves. Is he now chewing? Look at Sporho's flaming face. We both look back at the man's mouth. Knot on the man's throat bobs up and down. His dream about township bitches starts all over again, but this time his quick-fuck is the brooding girl. My mother Nomali is going to be happy and proud.

ENKUKWINI

Mother Nomali and my father Phung' Amanzi are reopening the garage. Malahla and Nkawu have gone deep into the township, passing out flyers, announcing the reopening. In the backyard, Nomali and Maya are treating the fire with plastic bags, logs, cardboards and lumps of coal. My father Phung' Amanzi carries a huge boxful of shoes and yellow and black banana peels. He drops it with a thud next to the now-heated fire whose twirling flames house a 50 litre container filled with water. He rushes to the storeroom, comes back carrying a bag of brown sugar and a big bar of yeast. Drops the bag and the bar. He coughs and walks away from the fire, waving away the specks of dust flying in front of his face. He stands in the shade his back against the wall of the house.

My mother Nomali empties the box of shoes and peels into the tank. Maya cuts open the bag of sugar with her long nails. She pours the sugar into the blend. Phung' Amanzi slices the bar in half and throws one half into the mix. Nxilandini and S'fombo bring potato and orange peels in a wheelbarrow. They help each other void their full pushcarts into the mix. My mother Nomali stirs the blend with her giant wooden spoon. For seven hours, it boils, thickens. Rotten smell rises in thick clouds, spreads across the yard, seeps through windows, doors, holes in the roof, cracks on the wall, to reach my nostrils in this drawer. A thick cloud of smoke hovers over the container as it boils.

Realising that I have nothing to contribute to cooking iBheya, my hatred for being stuck in this wardrobe intensifies. But at least am not the only one who does not have a role during the day. Bhogrom is barred from hanging around the yard during the day too. Mbulu is not allowed to be Mthimkhulu if he's to hang around the yard during the day and especially when iBheya is being boiled. This afternoon, he is a long-tailed black crow, nestled up in the corner of the cage outside the bedroom window. His tail drains the milk in the rusty trough. S'fombo keeps refilling it now and again as the sun beats down upon his wrinkled and dripping temples.

Nomali calls out Nxilandini and commands him to taste iBheya. He hesitates, iintsula zakhe fixed on the wooden bench near the gate. Phung' Amanzi waves his knobkerrie at Nxilandini. Jumps to his feet in fear, approaches the container with doubtful steps. Wish to laugh but I cannot find anything funny yet unless Phung' Amanzi starts beating up Nxilandini with his stick. The way he screams and shouts sorries always entertains me.

Neighbourhood never bothers interfering in our business. Smell of the boiling brew tingles the nostrils of the neighbourhood drunks. Can hear their noses sniffing the air, their parched throats making funny noises and roasting when they cough. Nxilandini cups, empties the liquid into a jug. Hotness of the jug burns his hands, but he fears Phung' Amanzi's hands enough not to drop and spill the brew. He finds a shade under the zebrawood.

At night, the tree curls its branches, its leaves shrink into little orbs, its protruding roots, which are feet, really, sink deep in the soil. Every passer-by sees a sleeping zebra, except the self- absorbed living. When the feet of the zebra have not been given water to drink during a hot day like now, it gives the neighbourhood insomnia with its snoring or wailing. This has gotten the people talking about some strange spirits living inside the zebra. They are wrong. Zebrawood yindlunkulu yoohili. Everyone knows about that morning when the neighbourhood brought big axes and saws and pangas and tried to chop the tree down. Didn't happen. Tree turned out harder than the weapons they had brought. Broke and melted all the axes and pangas and saws of the neighbourhood and deafened all those who tried to kill it. Heard my mother Nomali mocking and laughing at them for being so stupid not to know that getting drunk on her iBheya restores the hearing of those who have been deafened by the zebrawood.

Phung' Amanzi points and waves his fist at Nxilandini.

Voice yells: Don't sit near that tree, you dirty pig!

Nxilandini springs up, rushes to sit ngeempundu in the pouring heat of the sun, his back against Bhogrom's wooden cabin. He places the jug on the ground, waits for iBheya to cool down. Nxilandini panics, grabs the jug, pushes it near his mouth, blows and cools it with his lukewarm breath. Droplets of sweat fall into the jug. He begins sipping. Sighs, in-between sips. He downs the remainder of iBheya, drops the pitcher, his temples, sweat-dripping.

My mother Nomali shouts: Heh wethu, injani le Bheya?

Nxilandini does not answer, instead, staggers up, no balance. Hear the sound of iBheya boiling in his belly, readying to rush out his mouth or anus. He farts and belches. Eyes reddened flesh. He tries to walk towards Nomali, but trips, falls, his head hitting against a log. He opens his mouth. A scream and a gust of putrid breath jump out.

Phung' Amanzi spins his knobkerrie around in his right palm.

He says: This boy's head is weak. Just that one cup and he's this lame? Sies!

My mother Nomali laughs and then says: Hayi tata, iBheya istrongo kaloku. Bayithanda injalo kanye.

Malahla and Nkawu return empty-handed, their faces drenched in shining sweat, white overalls soaking wet, bodies tired. Don't understand how they get easily tired by simply walking. Sporho once told me human laziness is a sickness that nobody can get rid of. Wish I had their freedom of moving around during the day without the neighbourhood running away or chasing me like a strange beast. Close my left eye. Somewhere in my head there is a vague play of umkhwetha who has been beaten to death. He is hungry and his nqalathi has not brought him food for ten days. On the eleventh day, he can no longer stand the chopping blades of hunger, body drenched in ingceke, he walks down from Sakkiesdorp, enters Khaya township, and there he is sticked and stoned to death. Play fades away and the nail in my head rattles painfully and the play starts from scratch.

All our one hundred black and white cats come out of their cabin. March towards the front gate. Face the street and arrange themselves into a choir behind the fence. Standing on their hind legs, their open palms pushed forward, posture, penguinlike. Whenever iBheya is being prepared they come out, stand behind the wire fence, look at passers-by. Phung' Amanzi says the march of the cats brings good luck to the business. Only curious people from out of town stand still with wonder at our cats. Heard my mother Nomali telling my father Phung' Amanzi that the neighbourhood calls her Nokati. Phung' Amanzi said, And they call me Mfenana. Both chuckled and my mother Nomali smiled as if she liked the names.

Shepherds, except for Nxilandini, fill up over a hundred 1 litre plastic bottles with iBheya. It looks like glue in its thickness and hue. They store the bottled iBheya inside both the refrigerator and deep freezer. Garage has been swept clean and the chairs and tables arranged in a way that everyone who will be sitting down faces the counter.

Choir of cats turns around and the first row marches forward. The rest follow the lead. Walk gracefully into their wooden cabin. Door closes. Nobody knows what happens inside once the door shuts. Even Nokati has no clue. Think this might be what triggered Nxilandini's curiosity. He sneaked into the cabin. Ears heard a high-pitched yell. Then a strange silence fell and held the neighbourhood still. Cats pushed the iron door open, dragged Nxilandini out of their cabin. Left his scarred body in torn clothes sprawled near the zebrawood. His face was zigzagged with bloody marks. He could not speak for seven days. It was Mfenana who counted the scars and said to Nokati, He will be alright.

Drunks pour into our yard in droves. Fill up the garage with jabber, dense entjie smoke, the noise of clanking glasses, peals of laughter and lousy shouting.

Head spins and my nail jangles from all their noise in the garage and the panting of Nokati in the bedroom. Noise is so distractingly loud I can't help but look inside the bedroom. Nokati is bare, bending over the bed, hands spread out on the duvet, legs open to form an almost round bracket. Ntonga stands on top of three beer cases. He climbs the back of Nokati. Ntonga thrusts and drives umthondo wakhe into her like a screw into a piece of wood. He humps her like he's prepared to find out what uhili of Mambalwini experienced. So boring the tip of my nail does not tingle.

Look in the garage. Maya is holding a live chicken by its wings. Calm and poised, as though nothing is going to happen. Hate it when animals are like that, when they show no fear or panic in the face of death.

Three shepherds are serving bottles of iBheya to the excited drunks sitting at different tables. Nkawu serves his customers, placing iBheya bottles, on different tables. Then he walks towards the open garage door.

Almost evening and I cannot wait to be freed from this drawer. But that will only happen once Mfenana returns from feeding his seven black pigs ebuhlanti. Nkawu slides the door down. Sits down and joins the silent drunks that are staring at Maya. She is about to cut off the head of the white chicken with her long nails.

Maya's pinkie cuts the neck of the chicken. Room falls silent. Blood sprays out and marks the wall with death. Faces are marked with blood and yellow fluid. She places the dripping head on the counter. Body lies in a pool of blood in the middle of the table, making convulsive movements. Feel sick from these stupid tricks. Sickly long to be freed by Mfenana.

Chickenbody springs to his tiny feet. He jumps around and dances on the table. Drunks cheer and clap hands, shouting oohs and aahs in wonder. Chickenhead springs up, stands on his wounded throat. Shut up! Shut up! he shouts, voice hoarse. Room plunges into silence,

except for one drunk that keeps mumbling something about God's condemnation of sorcery.

You with no teeth shut up or I will tell news about your wife. Chickenhead's voice is tinged with aggression.

Drunk sits straight, sobers up. Chickenhead cackles, the garage shrinks with panic, the faces of the drunks like they have just seen Sporho. Surely they think it's the brew that is doing this to their eyes. Recall hearing Nokati telling Mfenana that the drunks believe that the brew is a hallucinogen. Sporho is right about the foolishness of the living.

Chickenhead entertains the drunks.

Once upon a time, he begins, *there were five white roaches. Four were men and one a woman. In their desperate search for food, they came across a brown corpse lying down near the Perseverance River.*

The roaches argued amongst themselves:

One said, *The arms are mine. I want to have strong muscles like him.*

The other said, *Both legs belong to me; I want to have strong legs like him.*

Another chipped in, *But my head is small, I'm taking his big head.*

Another said, *My tongue is short. I stammer, remember? I'm taking his long tongue.*

A squeaky voice said, *I want his big cock. My husband is small.*

Now, tell me, says Chickenhead, surveying the room while the body dances next to him, *what is the meaning of this scene, meaning of this scene, uh?*

Silence holds and tightens the room. Faces of drunks

redden and tongues toughen from not knowing what to say. Get sick with boredom from all their silliness. How can they miss the moral in this important tale? Tired of watching these foolish faces.

Inside the bedroom, Nokati is tucked in bed, her sweaty face protruding from beneath her black duvet, dreaming. Her dream interests me. A moment from my childhood memory.

Woman says: ukutya kwakho kusetafileni. Boy had bunked church that morning and gone to play TV games. He is now hungry and drenched in the stench of icuba, his lips are dry and white like ifutha on umkhwetha's body. He moves about and his clothes stink the house. It irritates his grandmother's nose as she mutters to his grandfather in the bedroom. His grandfather coughs and grumbles. Boy is sitting at the kitchen table finishing o' the piece of bread and downing it with umdoko. His mother pours cold water into the metal bathtub; brings out a bar of Sunlight and a metal scrub. His aunt comes out of her bedroom holding imvubu. Boy starts to feel pangs of pain cu!ing through him. A slightly hot wetness zigzags down his legs and plops on the kitchen floor. Grandmother limps out the bedroom armed with her dripping waslap. Boy shrieks as grandmother slaps his face left and back. He snorts out blood. His mother grabs and drags him by his scrawny neck and throws him into the bathtub. Water splashes and wets grandmother, and his mother, and aunt.

Boy's young brother laughs and says: undenza manzi! This makes them angry.

Imvubu lashes the boy's body.

Wet waslap slaps him across his face, cutting his cheeks.

Backhand klaps loosen his teeth.

Then the voice of his mother says: utshay' intsangu ngoku?

Another voice says: iqin' amasende le nkunkuma! Grandfather rushes out the bedroom. He says:

yinja engafun' nenkonzo le.

He punches the boy's mouth, blood sprays out. He shouts: ufun' ukufa?

Middle of the night, boy has stopped sobbing. His body itches, has contusions and sores. He scratches his arms, but can't reach his back. Body aches. He's tucked and hard-pressed between his mother and his young brother.

He hopes he does not urinate in bed again. Boy's noisy cat has returned. Meows squatting on a big cylinder container near the bedroom window. His mother wakes up. Flicks the lights on. Draws the curtains open, opens the windows, the wind blows in. The three avocado trees move to and fro hesitatingly. Boy wants the trees to smash the window in and scrub his back with their branches. His mother screams: huntshu nokatazana! Boy's cat does not flinch; it keeps meowing. He wants it to jump inside and scratch his back from force of habit. It stands on its hind legs. Claws at the broomstick as his mother waves it away. Meows and swirls around. Jumps and clings and swings on the electric cable. Boy gets off the bed and asks the cat to go away. Cat calms and gathers itself. Nods its head, strolls away.

His mother says: uyathakatha wena.

It begins to rain. His mother closes the window, then the curtains. She strolls out the bedroom. He hears clanking and crashing sounds from the kitchen. His young brother snores with his eyes wide open. Boy hears whisperings and giggles. Opens his eyes. His mother is standing over him. She beckons him to follow her into the kitchen. Lights in the TV room are out. Everyone is asleep except his mother and him. Rain has stopped. But the wind has begun screeching. In the kitchen, the boy sees himself cuddled at the corner, his face and hair are plastered with ingceke, and his eye-sockets are empty dark holes. He has no teeth, just black gums. Pot in front of him has been licked clean.

Boy tries to reach to himself and hug himself and tell himself that he misses himself but he can't move or open his mouth. He can't cry. He feels his eyes parching and swelling as though they want to blast out. Boy's lookalike stands up. He hangs in the air, a scarecrow, his feet not touching the ground. Boy stretches his arms to touch his lookalike but he flinches and disappears. Their mother yells: myeke!

UMRHOLISO

Nokati has run out of umgubo wonyamalalo. Usually, she climbs on a broom or a mop or any other object that obeys her voice and hovers. Then she rubs umgubo wonyamalalo behind her ears and sprinkles the powder on our heads and says the name of Bhakubha. Snaps her forefingers, vanishes right after shouting: Ntaba yentakatho Vul' amasango.

Spell works fast. Within seconds we drop from the sky and land on the bridge of bodies with skull-decorated pillars. Head dizzy, eyes hazy. Walk wobbly the narrow streets of Bhakubha. But, tonight, we climb, sit astride and ride Bhogrom's back, facing his arse. Nokati is holding his tail like it's a wheel. She is unsure if we will reach Bhakubha. She tells me her stomach has not got enough farts to help keep Bhogrom afloat when his body tires.

Bhogrom's back is big and wide enough to carry the two of us. His huge arms and legs coil and uncoil in a fast rhythm, springlike. He enjoys carrying us to Bhakubha. Suspect his willingness is brought about by the crescent moon and its delicate light. A full moonlit night drives him nuts. Bright blueness of the moon irritates his eyes, increases his bad temper, like that other night, when he refused to carry us into Bhakubha. Instead, he went about bellowing, beating his chest with one hand, dragging his chain with the other. His noise woke the neighbourhood. They simply watched as they could not do anything to stop it.

Nokati calls Bhogrom Swimmer. He plunges through the sky with force, although he gets tired too quickly. He still needs to work on his stamina and control the way he uses his energy in the air. Swimmer's wife, Mamfene, was better; she was swift and had an unbelievable stamina til one night, when Mbulu, Sihamba Ngenyanga, Mfenana and Nokati broke her back. Mamfene fell right before we arrived at the entrance point of Kwafindoda.

Nokati cast a spell: Moya wobumnyama Siph' ubuntaka!

Changed into black crows. We did not drop on the ground. Mamfene was too heavy and huge; she could not change into a bird. She fell flat and broke her back, limbs and neck. Surprised Swimmer has not refused us riding him yet he knows what happened to Mamfene.

In the black sky, we are in the company of vultures and owls and eagles. All harmless. In addition to enjoying being blown away by their speed, I revel in the manner in which the moon shines on our black bodies, the sensation of the cold wind of winter lashing our faces and mouths dry, the thickness of the clouds and how they scrape softly against our skins. Soar east towards Kwafindoda, cutting through bridges and boulders that turn out to be clouds. Dazzling stars seem so close and the earth a distant and vague land I cannot identify. Staring downwards, it's like we are suspended, still, in the black sky, watching heads, houses, motors in motion. After an hour or so of speeding, we slow down. Can tell Swimmer is weakening, groaning and shaking from tiredness.

Swimmer gives up a mile away from reaching the bush. He drops down his shoulders, his weakened arms, which no longer scoop and push the wind behind them. Legs are giving up. Our combined weights weigh him down. Body shivers with panic.

As we drop, my hands hold tight around his air-filled stomach. Nokati pushes iimpundu zakhe up, begins shooting out explosive farts after farts like firecrackers.

We hurtle through the windy sky fired and propelled by Nokati's bullets of wind.

Our landing in the bush gives Nokati a calf and a thigh strain.

Just glad it is not raining. Otherwise, we could have had a tougher time reaching Bhakubha.

Difficult to go against the heavy rain or wind when riding Swimmer. Easy to fall down and it is hard to rise back into the air.

Prefer the powder. Easiest way to get to Bhakubha. But Nokati must wait for seven days to refill her beaded bottle. That's only next week.

Nokati limps inside the clinic to service her hot arse and leg strain. Walk up the road, heading to the Black Hill where all amaBhakubha are gathered. Meeting is around Herd Boy – the kid ethwetyulwe by Mfenana and Mbulu on their way here. Mfenana says he suspects that it is Herd Boy who has been stealing his cattle and chickens.

In the courtyard, Herd Boy's body is tied to a pillar of skulls, arms and legs spread out, a crucified thief. Next to him are Mbulu and Mfenana, laughing at Herd Boy trying so hard to free himself. Unless he can fly or knows about the aloof umnga tree, he will never escape Bhakubha. Most people abathwetyulweyo have no clue about its existence. In the history of umnga tree, there is only one man who ran through it and escaped Bhakubha. But everyone knows who helped the man escape. It was the now dead Witch Mtha, a friend to Nokati. She did not take it well that she had to rholisa with her man though she knew the wages of failure. When she could not thwebula the daughter of tata Ngaka, am the one Gqwirha Elimhlophe sent to drag the man from his house to the bed of mud in Bhakubha. The tree is the only thing the living can use as a gateway to return to wherever they come from. But the Herd Boy does not really look like he knows anything, although there is something strange about his craggy face, which resembles that of the Rain-Maker.

Gqwirha Elimhlophe commands the two hyenas to slaughter the Herd Boy. The crouching hyenas rise and stand on their hind feet. Change into impish one- legged humanlike creatures endowed with two heads. Teeth, roughly apart, jagged, sawlike. They walk towards the pillar of skulls. Free the Herd Boy's tethered body and drag him through the gravel road. Drop him near the fireplace. Imbiza is boiling water. Onions and potatoes jump up and down inside the angry pot. AmaBhakubha are hungry. Rub their dry hands together, izinkcwe dripping down their mouths as the impish creatures make ready to slay Herd Boy for supper.

When they are done slitting his throat, cutting off his head, they chop the body and legs and arms into small portions. Throw the innards and pieces into the boiling pot. They approach Gqwirha Elimhlophe. Her iron forefinger nail prods their tails, changes them back into hyenas. Laane carries the Herd Boy's bristled head to the throne. Gains weight, becomes heavy, as he nears the throne. He drops the head near the fireplace. Calls out Butt Spencer, Sihamba Ngenyanga, Tero, Nomzamo and others to come help carry the head. But none of us can lift it off the earth or roll it. Heavy and unmovable.

Mfenana and other witches are angered. They begin shouting spells, the words of which I cannot catch. All their words hit the head and bounce back. Sound of the words against the head's flesh is louder than the useless screaming of the Herd Boy.

Head opens its mouth and eyes. We step back. Gqwirha Elimhlophe stands up; abandons her throne, something irregular and rare. Grootslange wake up and follow her steps, led by the shaken handmaidens. They all stand a few steps away from the head, which has grown so gigantic and gruff.

Head screams, Return my Rain Horns! Return my Rain Horns! Return my Rain Horns! His words travel so fast they are heard echoing in the depths of the bush.

In a minute, they come back to blast my ears and this irritates me so much.

Gqwirha Elimhlophe and the handmaidens all thunder laughter till the heavens heave and the ground grumbles. This angers the head. Eyes redden, hair changes colour. His breath parches, cracks the ground. Head turns into a boulder. Hurls itself about, smashing huts, destroying kraals, churches, dispersing amaB-hakubha, rolling over the stubborn. Sihamba Ngenyanga runs down the Black Hill, heading towards the red house. Hide behind the line of close-knit blue huts. But the head, as if it knows me, as if it has been watching me, rolls down behind my now-pedalling feet.

Trespass yards, tear down clothes hanging on lines,

jump through fences. Yelping dogs rush after me. Run much faster. Nail in my head rattles from the heat of it all. Head grows short legs. Chases. When the legs tire, they vanish and then the head rolls swiftly after me. Its speed disrupts the stillness of the ground. My pedaling feet feel light. Enter into an open green field. Discover that am no longer running on the gravel road. Am pedaling in the air. When I look down I see that almost everything has risen up – houses, huts, churches, clinics, stores even cattle, witches' familiars and amaBhakubha. Throne of Gqwirha Elimhlophe hovers. Only Persever-ance River and streams and the black corn fields are left on the landscape. Head becomes very angry. Gqwirha Elimhlophe, the handmaidens, and all the witches laugh and point at it mockingly.

Mtha did not kill the spirit of that Rain-Maker's husband! shouts the terrifying and loud voice of Gqwirha Elimhlophe, eyeballing Nokati.

Nokati stands leaning against the clinic, looking back at Gqwirha Elimhlophe.

When I saw the boy, I knew there was something wrong. Tat' uMfene, did not you sense something? asks Nokati's trembling lips, her fearful face, sweatsoaked.

Like everyone else I believed the spirit died with the body, says Mfenana, straddling umtshayelo, fixing his tobacco pipe.

We need the daughter of Ngaka. We need her blood and her head! Gqwirha Elimhlophe looks at Nokati. She's shivering. Do you want Bhakubha to eat your daughter? Nokati shakes her head, looks at me, her anger surges, blood boils, eyes bloodshot.

Gqwirha Elimhlophe shouts a spell: Ubunyama bakho mabubuyele kuwe!

Head turns back into flesh while it speedily rolls

about. When it realises that it is flesh it is too late to halt.
Can't quickly pace down. It smashes against the pillars of
skulls. For a while it closes its eyes, stuck against the
broken pillars, head buried in a heap of broken skulls. It
has a gash across its face. Hair is begrimed. After some-
time, it opens its left eye. Other one is completely closed.
Head sti'ens, wobbles, and the ground, too, follows its
rhythm. Then, water gushes through its ears, mouth and
nostrils. Giant waves of water splash and damage the
black corn fields, the fireplace, filling up the rivers, the
streams and the black sea level escalates. Head swells,
and then explodes. Massive waves jump and wet me,
Tero, Nomzamo, Bu! Spencer, Laane and many others,
except Gqwirha Elimhlophe, her handmaidens, her
Grootslange and witches and their familiars. They hover
above our heads, looking at the landscape that is now
covered with water in which debris, dead stumps, dirty
the surface.

It's not the last time the spirit visits. If we don't get
the blood and the head of Ngaka's daughter, *Bhakubha
will never rest.* Witches flinch at Gqwirha Elimhlophe's
words. None can ever enter or even hover over Ngaka's
house without being burned to death by his servant
uVutha. No single witch wishes to risk their life by going
to a house that even the tiny thieves of knowledge, the
messenger spirits, refuse to sneak into and spy.

Glide eastward for over an hour. Cold quivers my
body and chatters my teeth. Gqwirha Elimhlophe stops.
Beckons everyone and everything to descend.

AmaBhakubha and the witches and their familiars,
houses, huts, churches, cattle all settle on the ground.
Here, the moon wears the skin of a pale pig. All vegeta-
tion is vaguely green. Everything else – the way the
paths, streams and rivers are organised – is patterned

similarly to the old bush. Throne is the last to find its place up on the hillside.

Settles and overlooks Bhakubha. Down the valley, houses, huts, buildings, kraals spread out neatly under the moonlit sky. First thing amaBhakubha do after settling is find a fitting spot and put the pot next to a borehole. They gather dry bits and blocks of wood and start a fire, since everyone is feeling the biting cold waves of the night. Besides, their hunger has worsened. They talk among each other with sunken eyes and shaky stomachs. My own body, my throat, itch for iintsipho. Have not fed in a week. Now, my body is weakening and, whenever I have not had iintsipho for more than three days, my vision blurs, my limbs numb and tremble. There are unusual moments when none of these happen. Instead, all the memories I have about the east side of the township come alive in my head. Enjoy those short moments.

My eyes focus on what is going on up there in the hillside. Gqwirha Elimhlophe arises from her throne. Handmaidens and the Grootslange follow her as she moves about aimlessly. She finally stills, as if thinking, then, after a moment, her face relaxes. Points at Mfenana and Nokati and says: Every person you bring will be possessed by his spirit. Her eyes are inflamed with rage. You two must either bring the blood and head of that little bitch of Ngaka or we will sacrifice your daughter!

RIVER SPIRIT

Moon has withdrawn. Night pale and vague. Rain hails down, at first, in shiny bullets, unearthing earthworms. Then, it rolls down in splashes, intent on washing mud o' the tiny bodies of the writhing creatures, or bleaching ingceke put on my rubbery body. My skin has taken on the colour of ingceke. Not even the sharpest stone or the roughest steel wool can scrub it o' me. Stuck in this side of existence, my appearance is part of this experience.

Down the valley, amaBhakubha are figures on the run, each one hurrying into his or her own hut or house or shack, depending on their social status. Alongside the rushing river, listen to the rain flogging my flesh, a knobkerrie pounding a dirt-heavy mat. Feels like blade cuts. For the first time, in a very long while, stand still; look at isinyenye. All kinds of dirt has ingrained in the reddish scab. Has not completely healed, and yet it's not even sore anymore.

Sit down on a benchlike log; watch the rain fall and join the river's course. River water overflows, rushes as if hurrying to drown the world. Better if it were rushing to crack a hole in the screen. Nokati has put up as a barrier, barring me from entering the east side of the township. But the river does not know how to read minds. Does not have a mind. Has no other way of telling my wish, my inability to speak its language, nail rattling and mthondo-and-scrotum shrinking.

Want to tell the river about this downpour – how it rains memories into my head. Fragments of life in the east side of the township. Can only view the eastside if I stand on top of the giant rock on the hilltop. Even so, still can't clearly see the house where I used to live. It's hidden deep in the mess of huge houses and buildings. Eyes can't reach that far. A lot might have changed since the elders took me to entabeni. Wonder what the townshippers will say if they were to see me coming in my mkhwetha wear. Think they would welcome me. Not chase me away or try to trap me like those who want to lure me into snares. Surely they'll have to show respect; something more than what they show eza ntwana of Sakkiesdorp and Zanempilo.

Stand up from the bench. Move up the river. Rain is falling mildly. No longer violent. Raindrops are the tears of the Water Head. They say it does not die, but comes back every now and again, pestering like S'bhozo, til it gets what it wants. Gqwirha Elimhlophe will never allow Nokati and Mfenana to give back the Rain Horns. Moment that happens, the forever-gathering rain clouds will disappear, the fields will go dry. So will the rivers and streams and boreholes and creeks. It will be a plague straight from the earthen pots of the Rain Spirit, stripping of Gqwirha Elimhlophe's power.

Travel further up the river, the ground becomes dryer, raindrops warmer. Slowly, my body melts o' the gripping cold. Move with a strange force as though magnet is pulling me up to the beginning of the river. Not certain why am walking up this bank, but it seems to be something am supposed to be doing. Know that when the time arrives for us to leave for the township, Nokati and Mfenana will be looking for me all over the streets of our new Bhakubha. If they don't find me, can't imagine what kind of punishment my body will receive. When my feet reach the end of the embankment, the rain dissipates, the dark clouds clear, there are few stars beautifying the skyside. Air is dry and warm. Walk towards the jutting stone that oversees the palm tree whose roots stretch out to touch the mouth of the river.

Always wanted to know what will happen if my mouth go for days without feeding on iintsipho; without feeding on anything, not even on the black corn or oranges and wild mushrooms. Sneaked out while ezinye izithunzela were feeding in the room of iintsipho. Sure, when I stepped out, they all looked at me with careful eyes, questioning my decision of leaving the room whilst I have not had my share of iintsipho. Almost got into a fight with Bu! Spencer. He followed me around, reading my every step and turn, as if suspicious that am studying Bhakubha, looking for loopholes.

Sit on the flat stone facing the waters. One branch of the tree dangles and covers my face. Barely see what's in front of me. Doesn't maler. Just want to sit down, enjoy the memories that play at the back of my mind. After a while I find the branches in my face an annoying block-age. Can't have a clean view of the night. Grab the branch that blocks me from watching the rushing waters. Bend it. Breaks with a pleasing crack. Throw it into the river. Rush carries it eastward with the rest of the wreck. Look in the direction the water travels.

Wonder if ibhuma is still there. Maybe the elders of my township went there, did not find me, and thought I had drowned in the river. Decided to burn it down. Or maybe they never even went to fetch me. Out of fear of Kwafindoda's oddities. No ma!er what happens, will find out myself as soon as I know the right spell to break down the barrier.

Is that what you really want? a voice thunders from the waters.

Get up. Look carefully into the waters.

A figure appears, approaches me with a limp. Skin shines, lightens the night. I turn around and flinch. Pick up pace, heading back towards Bhakubha.

Nokati warned me about walking the distance of the bank. Said I should be watchful of the river spirits and run away if ever I come across them.

Stop, you who is lost, stop! shouts the figure.

Freeze. Can't move my feet. Look down – webbed and stuck in a thick spider net. Spider must be a really huge creature. First time seeing a spider net this thick and hard metallic wirelike. Wonder if this is the Rain-Maker, the ruler of the day, or simply a night trick of the river spirits. After all, the Rain-Maker has been slain and forgo!en long ago. Remember. Was Naliti who told me about the rain queen; when, where and how she had obtained her rainmaking medicines and herbs and how she met her death at the hands of Father Time. This was way before ilanga likaQilo.

You are right. I am not the Rain-Maker. Don't you know about the river spirits? I am one of them. My name is... not to be known by the enslaved.

Try to turn my head and look at the talking figure, but only manage to nod my head.

Why did you toss the branch into the waters without asking for permission from the river spirits?

Wish I had my tongue back.

Remember: Nokati never cooked mine. That purple thing I chewed and swallowed belonged to somebody else. She is keeping my tongue together nobumdaka bam.

Wish to speak back to the spirit so hard my chest aches.

Close my eyes. Spirit studies me for a while. Can feel the heaviness of the spirit's stare. Then the spirit says something in another language I can't grasp. Spider webs obey and dissolve into water. Throughout the spirit's tirade, look down, avoiding staring back and having my eyes and mouth twisted to the right side of my face. It is known that whenever encountering the people of the river, one is not allowed to talk or stare back. But after a while, realise that am not part of the living. Have nothing to fear for I have nothing to lose. Am already part of the world in which this spirit traverses. Stare back. Four-breasted woman, skin made of water.

You have disturbed the sprits, the woman says. You must do one thing for the spirits of the waters.

Look at her milky eyes. She is nothing like the women I have seen in my memory of the township. Her body and face and voice – nothing like the women in Bhakubha.

Nod at her.

The spirits know you are lost. Bring and sink the Rain Horns in this river. The spirits will open the east-side for you. Woman turns around, approaches the river-mouth, and disappears into the rushing waters.

Rain Horns are hanging in the bedroom of Nokati. Not sure if I can steal and bring them here. Wonder what

Nokati and Mfenana would say or do if they ever found out that I had stolen the Rain Horns. Mfenana told me the reason Bu! Spencer and Tero and Nomzamo and Laane can never go back into the township. Attempted to steal the Rain Horns, were caught and cursed to slave in the bush of Bhakubha forever.

UMPHANGA

Datsun parks in front of our wooden gate. Shakes for a moment, coughs out a gust of black smoke, noisy engine collapses. Next door neighbours, the old woman (who was struck dumb and deaf by the zebrawood after gossiping in the township that Mfenana 'uthwala ngeehagu ezimnyama') and her daughter, turn their heads and rove their eyes. Old woman stops sweeping the yard, her daughter stops hanging the clothes on the line. Their bodies freeze, stares probe the car. Windows of the car are grimy, the tyres and doors are caked with dry mud and dust.

Car doors are pushed open. Gospel music springs out, fills our yard and house with a bassy sound. Windows and the tin roof rattle. Song irritates me with its halfsermonising, halfpraising lyrics. Bassy music is a hand shaking the nail in my head, widening its hole. Feel the hurt, curse the noisy music til it dies.

Mother and Father. Their thoughtful look is what grips me though I can't make out how they feel. Legs climb out the Datsun.

My mood changes. Feel confused and scared. Sporho's image comes to mind. Promised him I would not abandon him. Told him I will be there beside him to play Death when the night has stopped carrying a crescent moon.

That's when Nokati is going to heal. She needs me to accompany her to attend the Blood Festival. Nothing I can do about my imprisonment. Have to wait til Nokati recovers. Til then am locked, bored in this wardrobe, day and night, a beast that knows no sleep.

Sporho's face haunts me.

In my head he appears and disappears as I think about what Mother and Father have come here to do.

He's not happy, his bony face is bloodstained, opens his tongueless mouth, blood floods out.

Abruptly open my eyes. Car doors shut close.

Mother and Father walk into our yard.

Father hits the door with two knocks, steps back and waits for a response.

Mother whispers into Father's right ear. He smiles and plunges his left hand into the left pocket of his trousers. Pulls out an asthma pump, shoves it into Mother's mouth.

She pumps, inhales, pumps, inhales. Father gives the door another two knocks.

Ngaka told them am here. He is the only one owuchanayo umhlola in this entire township and is known to have helped lots of people that were bewitched or poisoned.

Must be Ngaka who sent them, because, last month Vutha walked into our house, face enflamed with fury, breath burning all flies in sight. Nokati was tucked in bed, sweating and snoring. Vutha removed the blankets. His hot hands hugged and held Nokati's big feet til they heated and caught fire. Vutha vanished, leaving the floor riddled with flaming footprints, and the room darkening with smoke.

Nokati opened her eyes, choked on the gust of smoke, jumped o' bed, screaming, Ndiyatsha! Ndiyatsha! Nceda! Paced the house bumping and breaking things. Hurled her body to the floor, rolled around mumbling mixed-up sentences, but the fire would not die out.

Mfenana came back running from the toilet. Rushed inside the house, zipped and belted his bhrukhwe. Saw Nokati's legs on fire. Open the windows. From the mantelshelf (packed with all kinds of boilled herbs), Mfenana grabbed a bottle of uZifo Zonke mixed with charcoal and another white powder whose name I have forgotten. He shouted, Cima! Cima! Cima! Sprinkled the mix over her head. He doused out the flames before they could reach Nokati's breasts. It came to me that someone, an enemy of the family, must have gone to get help from Ngaka. Only Ngaka's Vutha is strong enough to burn Mfenana and Nokati. Believe Ngaka has given Mother and Father the power to come free me from the weariness of this wardrobe.

Ngaphakathi! Nokati shouts.

Her voice is husky, tone tinged with annoyance. Whizzes from the kitchen, dies after reaching the ears in the living room. She twists her face in pain and fear, trembles her lips, twitches her eyelids. She has begun chopping the onion into jagged blocks; her eyes are dripping wet, nose runny. Hearing heightened, the sound of the chopping blade against the hardness of the table is so loud and lousy and grating.

Father turns the latch left opens the door and enters the house.

Mother follows behind with doubtful steps, uneasiness on her face.

They stand next to the craggy mantelpiece, look at the semidark passage ahead, wait for someone to appear from somewhere and command them to sit down.

Look who is at the door, Nokati says to Maya. Maya drops the plastic plate in the sink. Grabs a rag and dries her foamed hands. Tosses the rag on the table. Drags her flip-flops across the newly tiled floor. In the living room, Mother and Father meet Maya's eyes. If she is not shocked to see them here, she is scared that Mother and Father might know am here. They have come to return me. This is what has frozen her on her feet.

She stares, mouth does not say anything, but her worried face reveals her shaken spirit. Many minutes pass. Maya is still staring at Mother and Father. They have not moved their legs or lips. Wonder why they have not brought the police with them. Know they went to report that am missing. Seen posters on the street with an image of me smiling, head shaven and face ngcekeed. Sporho and I used to tear these down with hatred.

Nokati shouts: Ngubani lowo? Her voice is hoarse, tone is harsh.

Mama! Mama! Ngaa – Ngaa – Ngaa...Tears well in Maya's huge eyes, but she manages to hold them back. She does not want to break down in front of Mother and Father.

She gathers herself. Chest swells with air.

Arms akimbo.

At last, the words blast out, Ngabazali bakhe, *Mama*! Maya's roaming eyes, as she stands with her back leaning gently against the tall grandfather's clock, say to me that this is the reason she's filled with fear or shock or pain and this thought enlivens me.

Wonder if her shock or fear or pain is not caused by the realisation that in two weeks it's the Blood Festival. Her mother has not attempted to capture the daughter of Ngaka. Remember what Gqwirha Elimhlophe said to Nokati about the daughter of Ngaka and Maya. Maya knows that Nokati has run out of ideas. Nokati does not know how to ensnare Ngaka's daughter. Nobody seems to know how. Nokati, like her dead friend, who was forced to sacrifice her husband, after failure to capture Ngaka's daughter, knows the wages of failure. Shaking has stricken Nokati's goosebumped body.

She stops humming, stares through the round little window in the kitchen, captivated by the neatness of our backyard. Shepherds have cleaned it and discarded all the stinking rubbish that has been collecting and piling up near the toilet. Not hard to see that Nokati is wondering about Father and Mother. Sense fear surging inside her. Never seen Nokati so shaken and scared before. Vutha has made her timid. Mfenana has been talking about Mother and Father. Saying that one day Mother and Father will discover my whereabouts. It will be too late. They won't be able to do anything about their finding. This is the moment Mfenana and Nokati were talking about. Nokati seems to be thinking about this very maler. Maybe she is convinced that it's Mother and Father who sent Vutha.

Nokati limps to the living room. Her body is still painful from the burns of Vutha. She is much better now, though. Can see in the way she carries herself and how she pushes her steps that she still feels a pain. Not long ago, she could not walk or wave hands or nod her head. She could only talk when asleep. Senseless sentences slipped out her mouth, peppered with people's names. Ones I remember are – Nyathel' Igqwirha, Nodada,

Ndofaya, Ntsapho, Nokwakha, Nkundla, Mother and Father. These names belong to the parents of friends that work in Bhakubha. Think Nokati has been cursed or condemned. She has a habit of walking in her sleep, shouting all these names aloud and breaking down in a hysterical wailing. Mfenana did not sleep the whole of last month. He had to stay awake to keep her from walking out the house. He locked her up in the bedroom, played the music loud, so the neighbours would not hear her hysterical shouting, outbursts of laughter and floor-cracking stamping. Attimes, especially in the morning, when Mfenana is out to feed his black pigs and get his body licked by their white tongues, she punches the wall til it cracks and her fists bleed. Watch her lick her hurt fingers to sleep during these mad moments. It's true that once Vutha has not killed someone, he leaves them su'ering.

Nokati holds a plate in one hand, a dry rag in the other, swinging her hips in an arrogant gait. She sees

Mother and Father, then; hiding her shock, she coughs. Her coughing lasts for many minutes.

Water, bring water bring water, please. Nokati points the plate and rag to Maya. Maya takes them and walks to the kitchen. She keeps looking back, feeling she's being followed or looked at. Clock ticks slow. Maya brings a jug of cold water and hands it over to Nokati. She drinks half the water, gives the jug back to Maya. She grabs the pitcher and disappears into the kitchen. Nokati looks at Mother and Father and then says: Why are you not sitting? Are your arses on fire?

On the couch, Mother and Father sit next to each other.

Nokati stands erect. She talks and rubs a salve on her wrists.

Wonder why she mentions fire. Maybe she is giving them a clue – letting them know that she knows they went to ask Ngaka to send his servant Vutha to burn Nokati to death.

Mother and Father are quietly staring at the chatterbox Nokati. Nothing about their sitting postures or facial expressions says they know the things Nokati knows.

What do you want? Nokati's voice is harsh, face creased with disgust.

Mother and Father look at each other for the longest time, each refusing the responsibility of explaining their visit. Their eyes are swelling with tears. They are trying very hard to hold the tears back. They confuse me. Can't tell if they are acting or being serious, so their seeming sadness does not affect me.

Kwenzeka ntoni apha? says Nokati, rolling her eyes.

Her couch faces Mother and Father. They are still, silent and sullen.

Nokati claps her hands loudly and continues: The boldness! Hehehehehe hayini! You killed my daughter and come to my house and pretend you are deaf?

Nokati slides off the couch, drops down ngeempundu, remains sitting, her unfriendly stare directed at the faces of Mother and Father.

She claps her hands twice and shakes her head. She sighs, struggles to stand up. With both hands, she holds the arm of the couch near her. She pushes her hands hard against the arm of the couch, pushes her body up. Strain is written on her wrenching face. Finally, she manages to stand up.

Father's throaty voice falters. Can...uh... can, uh, he struggles. He clears his throat and coughs twice. Can we talk to the whole family? Before Nokati responds,

Mother, her hands rubbing her knees, looking Nokati in the eyes, says, O sisi wam! We did not come to reopen and salt old wounds.

Nokati remains quiet for minutes long. Mother and Father are not touched by this. Can't they see that this is a way of being told they are not welcome in our house? Annoys me that they are stalling to open their mouths, to get to the truth. Return me to Khayamnandi if that's what they are here for. Unsure about going with them though I'd do anything to see my brothers. No longer care about being the first Man in the townships, to have umgidi woqobo in 500 years. Think about Sporho and wonder how he is going to know that I've gone home, if I leave with Mother and Father. Get more confused as I think hard about this mater. Harder I think about this, the more my nail rattles and my head and chest heat up. Cool my head down by indulging a memory that comes to mind.

One night, a week before the elders took me to Kwafind-oda, near the Daleview Bridge, an owl shadowed me through the dark mountainous streets, stinging my ears, with its intolerable hooting. Walked up and there were few people rushing in the opposite direction of Lang Straat. Was dead sure they were all sleeprushing through the empty street. They could neither hear the hooting nor see the owl. Came to a street with brightly lit lamps. People kept rushing, black bodies, unbothered by noth-ing. Stopped, turned my head back to check why the hooting owl had muted its torturous noise. Noticed that it had disappeared. Was all alone with the funereal night, whose windy darkness summoned plastic bags and papers to circle in a dusty whirlwind behind me.

By the time I finally arrived at home, my ears were bleeding and hurting. Suspected that the owl had stopped stalking me when I came to Reservoir Hills, whose streets are nightly glimmering with yellowness, conjured by the big and bright streetlights.

Surprised that I remember this moment and how it made me feel. If I go on for longer and dodge the feeding period, I might remember everything, including my brothers' names, which I have forgotten. Nothing beats the entertainment of enjoying fragments of memories, inside this wearisome wardrobe, whose stale stench irritates my throat.

Nokati remains quiet. After a while, she shakes her head, says, Maya, my child, come here asseblief. Nokati coughs. It lasts for only a minute, a feigned cough. Maya comes running from the bedroom. She stands before Nokati, bends her head and body over. Her hands touch the arm of the couch. She closes her eyes. Nokati whispers into Maya's ear. Maya stands up straight. Walks out of the house, steps out the yard, into the peopled street.

She returns, followed by the slow steps of Mfenana. His face is bloated with irritation. He hates being distracted. Ask Nkawu and S'fombo, he beat their faces til the flesh was broken and swollen. He told them to never distract him while he's feeding his beloved black pigs. Mfenana knows that he is nothing without the pigs. Everyone knows it's those pigs that lick his body so that he remains healthy and young. How and where he got the pigs, nobody knows, nobody cares to find out. Even his aging peers who envy his youthfulness don't bother finding out.

He sits down on the empty couch next to Nokati and starts fixing his tobacco pipe.

We thought to let you know, begins Father, rubbing his hands between his thighs.

His crotch is bulging, a small bag overstuffed. His eyes are glassy.

His mouth moves and these words roll out: We are burying my son this Saturday!

Mother bows her head. Takes off her specs. Her eyes have swollen and reddened. She pushes her handkerchief to her eyes, rubs the thing against them. Heart feels crushed and my head and eyes are searing and I cannot fight o' the pain in Mother's eyes. O Mother, O Mother! I would like to scream. Remember that I have no tongue; cannot move out of this wardrobe. Feel my heart being ripped out of my chest. Place where my heart is situated is a bottomless hole.

The police fished his body out of the Uitenhage River, Father's now soft voice says.

His tired eyes fixed on the frigid faces of Nokati and Mfenana.

Father covers his mouth with his handkerchief holding hand. Coughs and spits into the kerchief. Folds and tucks the thing into his trouser pocket.

His head falls and hangs on his chest.

His left arm is wrapped around his head; his wrist touches his right ear.

Mother begins, This is my son's graduation year, you know. Her voice is shaky.

She stops talking, chokes on tears. Father brushes Mother's left knee.

He uses his other hand to wipe Mother's wet face.

After a while, Mother looks at Nokati, says, I am sorry about your daughter, sisi.

Nokati sighs and looks at Mfenana.

Mfenana empties his tobacco pipe on his palm.

Smears the ashes on his head.

Look at their mouths. Confused as to why they are talking about me as if am not here. Mother starts weeping. Father grabs and holds her close to his chest. Feel maddened at the way they talk about me as if am dead. The way they believe that it is me whom the police have fished out of the river. Not angry, just annoyed. Want to laugh the lousy laugh. Laugh at them for saying that they have found me dead and are going to bury me this Saturday. Ridiculous! Sick! Did not they see that the body is not mine? Mother, Father, and my brothers, did not they notice that there is something wrong with the way that body looks? Mandy, she would have pointed out that the body is not mine. She knew every birthmark or blemish on my body. She would have pointed out each birthmark or blemish, described how each looks, eyes-closed.

Mfenana coughs. Smokes his pipe, pulling in lungful of smoke, holds his breath for a moment. Breathe thick, grey clouds through his hairy nostrils. Mother and Father choke and cough, their faces darkening with disgust, hands waving away the pipesmoke.

He stares at Father and Mother, says, I hear you. Oohlathi have forgiven you. He looks at Nokati, voice adds, What do you say? Did not we forgive them long ago?

Nokati nods. She twists and turns her face in pretence. Can't they see she does not feel hurt by my fake death? Annoyance subsides, only for the anger to rise. Feel it boiling in my gut. Remember that she told me at Mandy's funeral that my life will never amount to anything. This is my existence and what it has amounted to: imprisoned in this wardrobe, with no right to social life. Want to get out of this wardrobe and smash their snouts in, break their limbs and run away with Mother and Father to live again with my brothers.

We'll try to make it to the funeral, Nokati's twisted-mouth says coldly.

Look at Father and vague images of my brothers flash through my head. Feel strange, partly relieved and half-angry that Mother and Father have not come here to return me. They will never return a tongueless beast to stay among the living. They will never accept me. Think about Sporho and how bored he must be in his grave. I love him because he understands how it feels to be trapped in a cramped space the whole day without social life.

Mother and Father stand up. Without announcing, they stomp out the house. Mfenana and Nokati and Maya burst into a laugh. Can see that the laugh is not a real one. They are just making themselves feel better. They thought that Mother and Father know that am trapped in this wardrobe. That is all. It's not like they have discovered a way of tricking Ngaka's daughter into captivity. Only thing that instils hope in my heart is that one day I will escape this entrapment, make my way home. One day is during the nearing Blood Festival.

Arrival of the two deaf, dumb little girls kills the excitement in the room. The two brats drop their bags at the stoep. Rush into the house, headed for the kitchen. They soon discover that Nokati has not cooked. Pots smell of Sunlight soap. Kitchen floor has been swept and the smell of impepho hangs in the air in a thick cloud. The twins confront their mother. The older-looking twin bloats her stomach. She points to it with fingers, indicating she is hungry. Nokati stays quiet, slips her hand in her purse. Pulls out a twenty rand note, says, Maya, go get bread for your sisters.

Maya does not hesitate. Grabs the money from Nokati's hands, walks ahead and bangs the door behind her butt. Mfenana stands up and looks at Nokati for a long time. He shakes his head. Steps out the house, followed by his big black mongrel.

Think of Laane. His family had to bury an empty coffin when they could not find his body. Riverin Uitenhage refused to spit him out. Naliti told me that Laane's family should not have cried when they heard that he had drowned. After the burial of his coffin he began visiting his house, tossing and breaking things in the darkness of the kitchen. It was Ngaka who helped stop Laane's violent visitations. Stepped out his house, carrying a stu'ed bag made of leopard skin. Walked up into the dense night of Kwafindoda bush. Spent a night there, though nobody knows what he was doing and how he survived alone in that haven of *witches and wicked spirits*. Rushed down the following morning, his face bloody, clothes tattered, shouting throughout the streets of Khayamnandi, I have slain the shadow! I have slain the shadow! I have slain the boy's shadow!

INKUNGU

Fog refuses to go away. Sun has not been rising in the township. It's been foggy the entire week, and it's impossible to separate day from night. The two deaf, dumb twins have not been attending school. Have not been playing outside. Nokati is extra careful. She says they might get lost in the fog and never be found again. They cannot attend school or play outside when cars and cattle cannot move because wandering sprits are flooding, blocking the streets. There have been lots of accidents and crashes. Hear reports on the radio, see casualties on TV. A week ago, a truck drove straight into a wall of an RDP house somewhere here in the township, house collapsed, whole family died in their sleep. This happened right after Mfenana left the house. Fog began falling in droplets of ice. It was not long and the entire township was pale. Soon people were banned from being outside their houses.

Shops closed down. News says they are being robbed. Clinics and schools have been shut down, too. I know the real reason why they all have shut down, but the news will not report the truth, for fear of scaring the townshippers. They won't tell about the bodies of other townshippers that are being discovered, every hour, in different parts of the townships. All of them die the same death – their bodies sucked dry, eyes emptied, genitals and tongues cut out.

Doubt townshippers believe what the news tells them. At night, the unbearable noise of screams and moans and shouts set ears and heads on fire. Fog thickens each day, each night. See it pushing its thick clouds against the window, trying to break into our house. But Nokati has mixed herbs and liquids, smeared the concoction on the insides of the windows and doors. Fog cannot get inside. Windows only sweat. Impossible to see through them. Appear to be drenched in thick white paint.

Our house feels like it's situated in the middle of a bush. We are the only people here. Surrounded by a thick blanket of white fog. Silence subsumes the house, makes me believe that our house is in the middle of Kwafindoda. Absence of booming music from the tavern down the street, of tooting taxis and drunken din, makes me suspicious. If it were not for the news that plays now and again, showing what's happening in the other parts of the township, I would go on believing that everyone else has been killed in this community. TV plays the same, unchanging news. Reports nothing new. All it gives us is lies. Know they are fabrications because I think I understand the thing that is happening. Blood Festival is nearing. That's why Nokati has been ill-tempered, Maya miserable, Mfenana, Mbulu and Bhogrom missing.

Mfenana has not come home from feeding his black pigs. It's been a week. Nokati is not allowed to go near ebuhlanti. Women are not permitted ebuhlanti or in Kwafindoda. Maya is the only woman who is bold enough to walk into ebuhlanti to get Mfenana whenever there is an emergency at home. Boys and men of Khayamnandi Township fear and respect her and call her Nongayindoda, because, they say, she is built tough, indomitable and has the strength of a Man.

Shepherds are drunk on iBheya; they have not gone home since the afternoon fog began falling. They are locked up in the cabin opposite Bhogrom's apartment. Mfenana hates distractions, especially when he is working ebuhlanti. Nokati does not want to send the shepherds to look for Mfenana. She shows no signs of worry about his absence. Maya is the only one who is worried about him. She asks her mother about Mfenana.

Displeased, Nokati points her index finger at Maya and shouts, Hamb' onya wena!

She has been very irritable lately, and has taken a liking to throwing insults at me. If she is not insulting my failed manhood, Nokati mocks Mother's loose and stinking bhentse and Father's small and useless ncanca.

I told him not to attend that funeral, says the bubble-gum-chewing mouth of Maya, her huge eyes studying the whiteness of the window.

Don't talk about things you don't know! Nokati snaps. She is kneading dough in a big brown bowl. It sits in the middle of the rickety kitchen table. Maya is sitting on a chair next to the shut door. At her feet, the twins are playing with their blue-eyed dolls. Remember, as umkhwetha, I dreamed about toy guns and blue-eyed dolls.

That whole month I had the same dream:

A cluster of young boys and girls play noisily. Young boys

brandish toy guns and tiny cars and trucks. Young girls are
pissed o' as they repeated- ly punch their blue-eyed dolls.
Sticking the dolls out in the sky, singing 'dead dolls, dead
dolls, dead dolls'. It always ends with me at some corner
collecting plastic bags and papers and dregs of rubbish to start
a fire. The fire burns for a while. I curse and spit into the fire.
Pull out umthondo, quench the fire with urine.

Nokati believes it's a bad omen to open the door during a foggy day or night when the man of the house has not returned from ebuhlanti. It's Maya who has been challenging this rule, asking what if Mfenana had gotten in trouble and needs help? Nokati has been insistent. She does not want to go against a tradition that has been placed by the ancestors.

Mama! The ancestors have been dead for a long time. How are they going to help him? Maya looks at Nokati coldly and coughs.

Nokati points at Maya with fingers sticky with dough. She shouts, Don't talk bad about your ancestors, rubbishkazi yomntwana!

If he does not come back, what are we going to do, Mama? Nokati remains quiet. Can see in the way she palms and fists the dough that Maya is angering her, but she is trying very hard to keep calm.

Do you think his mother and father sent you uVutha, Mama? Maya is working hard to get on the nerves of Nokati and their whole talk begins to annoy me greatly. Indifferent as to whether Mfenana comes back or not. It will have no impact on me. Don't see why I should be listening to this nonsense. Don't know how many times Mfenana has disappeared, returning after three or four days telling a tale about how he had been kidnapped by the spirits of the bush while making his way home.

I think they know he is here, continues Maya her eyes fixed on her mother's upset face. After some time, Nokati yells, Shut up, Maya! Don't be stupid! Then Nokati covers the dough with a white cloth. She places the bowl next to the microwave. Switches the radio on, fiddles with the knob and runs through different stations. Stops turning the knob when she finds a station that plays Gospel music. Annoys me so much I wish I had a way of stepping out the wardrobe and running away. Come back when the radio is playing something interesting, imiphanga or reports on number of deaths in the fog.

You'll make dumplings for supper? Nokati's voice is now soft. She tries to be sweet with Maya. Mouth wants to laugh my brother's lousy laugh. Bhakubha will have Maya as supper. Nokati and Phung' Amanzi will never get hold of Ngaka's daughter unless they kill him. Ngaka is said to have lived and survived decades and no one knows his age. None of the people in all three townships in Despatch know him personally. Nobody remembers where he came from, when he arrived here. Nobody has seen his face. He wears a mask, in a dark room, during interaction with the sick who seek help from him. People only hear stories about his beautiful and long-haired daughter.

It was Naliti who first told me that the blood of the daughter of Ngaka is dangerously important. That it is impossible to see that woman outside Ngaka's house, because the witches want her head and blood, so she remains hidden in Ngaka's bunker, imimoya safeguarding her existence.

Maya does not respond to her mother's words. Maya knows that her time has come. No hideout or escape routes. She must accept the wages of failure, or Gqwirha

Elimhlophe will turn all her siblings into cockroaches and crush them to death. Look at their heavy eyelids. Mouth wants to laugh at their misery. Maya seems entranced by something. Can't say if it's something on the street that is holding her attention. Window does not allow her to see through it. Streets are obviously empty and quiet anyway.

Look at the Rain Horns that hang on the hanger behind the wooden door. Mfenana has moved the Rain Horns here in this kitchen. Think he was afraid that, in her hysterics, Nokati might grab the Rain Horns and hurt herself. Sick people should not go near the Rain Horns, said Mfenana when he was removing them from the bedroom. Think of ways of stealing them without being noticed. It would be great to have the barrier broken down, to visit the eastside of the township whenever I want without Mfenana and Nokati knowing. Go see my brothers. Come back to play Death with my friend Sporho.

After a while, Maya, looking in her mother's eyes, says, What are you going to do, Mama? Are you going to allow them to take me? Nokati sighs, sinks into silence. Sneezes, closes her eyes, for a long time. Maya leaves the kitchen, walks towards her bedroom. Close my eyes.

Image of Mother and Father holding hands and smiling appears in my mind. Remember staring at the picture as it hung on the wall of their dining room. It was on the day the elders took me to Kwafindoda. Remember small things –scattered photos and cards on the table. Have not had iintsipho in the longest of time. Feel a difference; something in my head, my heart, a feeling I have not felt in a while. Wish Mother and Father were here. Would hold them close to my chest tightly, never let them go.

Imagine how my funeral went down. Only a few townshippers would have attended.

Was never the beloved of my township. Close my eyes for such a long time that I forget my eyes are closed. An image, a memory of a dream, returns to me with vividness. As umkhwetha, I used to have it often during my time in Kwafindoda. I'd dream that I was ebhumeni, my body strapped and tied to a decaying log, and ibhuma filled with duplicates of Nokati's naked body. Could not breathe, could not scream. Bodies would multiply, pile up on top of my thin frame, their laugh making me nervous. With all the bodies of townshippers that are being discovered every hour, I wonder if the dream am remembering now is not somehow connected to these deaths. If so, what is the connection, the significance? A sign? For what and why? Can't be chance that am remembering this dream at this moment.

Open my eyes. Nokati has collapsed on the couch, deep in sleep. She's worrysick. Maya is siling on the chair in the kitchen, staring and studying the window again. The twins are now playing upuca – each girl clutches a group of pebbles in her right hand. The young-glooking twin throws a pebble in the air. When the pebble descends, grabs the rest of the stones (grouped on the floor inside a box drawn of white chalk) closer to her left leg.

Something in the twins' eyes. Have not noticed this before. Maybe it is something completely new, brought by the absence of Mfenana and the anxiety that has stricken Maya. Nokati has fallen deep into indifference. Or at least she pretends. Can't tell the difference. Eyes of the twins are white. Roll and orbit in their sockets, spinning milky marbles. Wonder how Nokati would feel if these two things got killed or kidnapped, their bodies discovered somewhere in a township corner, like all the township corner, like all the townshippers whose lives are worth nothing. Sure nobody cries for them at their funerals. Funerals are parties – nobody has time to cry. People laugh and get drunk and dance. Nobody cried for me at mine, I imagine. All there was at my funeral was joy and happiness. How could the township not be happy? Was going to be the first Man to have umgidi woqobo, in 500 years! Umgidi wam would have been overcrowded... My nail rattles...remember that am wasting my energy thinking of things that would never occur. Trapped here now because of the envy that has struck the township.

Shut my eyes. All I see is a fog. A cloud of whiteness has taken over my head. How did it get into my head? Thought the herbs and liquids Nokati mixed were of help. The concoction only works against the fog invading the house, I guess. Maybe the fog has invaded Nokati's head too. Maybe it is the reason she no longer dreams. Have not heard her saying anything in her sleep. Have not seen any images in her head. Her mind is a clean white sheet. What about the foggy eyes of the twins? A connection here. Maybe their eyes have not always been this white. Fog painted them white. Can't wait for the fog to disappear. It is making the lives of everyone hard. Would be a relief to be able to sleep or dream. Would be the best way to deal with this silence and irritating fog. It invades everything but our house. Try to trick the part of my mind that is responsible for dreams and sleep. Have not slept or dreamed in a long time. Last time I slept or dreamed was in Kwafindoda. Want to remember how it feels to dream or sleep. Try again. Focus hard on any memory I can recall that involves me either sleeping or dreaming. Nothing comes to mind, my mind refuses to be tricked.

Open my eyes. Have not seen Mbulu and Sporho and Bhogrom. Wonder. Maybe they have disappeared with Mfenana. Things like that happen. Maybe Mbulu and Bhogrom are keeping him company ebuhlanti. It's possible. Don't believe that something bad has happened to Mfenana. His life or death means nothing to me. Want to see Sporho. Look at the Rain Horns hanging behind the kitchen door. Nail rattles with angst and anger. Would be easy to grab them. Impossible is freeing myself from this entrapment. Have no spell to grant me control over my movements.

RETURN

Peep through the window. Uncertain if it is morning or evening. Can't tell the difference. Suspect it is evening for the fog is slowly drifting, thinning away, a sign that the witches have landed in Bhakubha. This kind of fog has always been a decoy. Empties and quietens the township, sweeping the streets of all those who go about like desperate dogs. Shocked that there is no sign of the whirlwind. Usually, the fog falls, spreads thickly over the earth – a white blanket that mistifies everything. After a while, the whirlwind is expected to wreak mayhem. Has become clear that no such occurrence will follow.

Fog slowly melts into dew. Has already soaked objects and stones outside. Windows too, are steaming, sweating excessively. See through the bedroom window how the fog travels further towards the bush. Many people don't know that this fog is witchbrewed in imbiza. An altar for that in Bhakubha. Gluey brew is used to render the witches invisible. They travel from all over the place to a!end the Blood Festival. Happens twice a year. Visiting witches have now landed in Bhakubha, says the thinning away fog, but the arrogant living cannot understand this revelation.

Been feeling sick from all the memories of home, the eastside of the township, that have been visiting me. They appear, disappear and reappear, Sporholike. Nail rattles. Forced to close my eyes, my vision blurs. What haunts me horribly are the faces of Mother, Father, brothers and everyone else I know. Rainy; faces and feet are drenched in mud. They all laugh as my coffin descends into the gaping hole. Same image comes back each moment my eyes close – a thought-track I cannot control. Lost track of time. Usually very conscious of time, cos there is nothing to do here but study the clock. Still my thoughts, listen to the snoring twins and Nokati, while I watch the movement of the hands of the huge wall clock. In the kitchen, Maya goes up and down, nerve-wracked, face sweating and arms trembling.

Bhakubha is jumping up and down with great appetite, cleaning their teeth, licking their lips, detoxing their stomachs, readying themselves for tonight's festival. After much aimless pacing, Maya stops at the kitchen window, stares through it. Zebrawood has begun wailing. Branches are shaking. No wind or breeze. Shaking is not from the tree being unfed. Nokati has been alending the roots of the tree the entire time. Tree is missing Phung' Amanzi. Wailing sounds very different from the tree's usual wailing when it is thirsty for water. Now it is a broken instrument that produces an irritating noise, setting my head and ears on fire. Noise has entered my head, rattles the nail with its sharp racket, and my eyes burn from the hot head produced by the din of the zebrawood. Noise booms in bassy waves that trembles the asbestos roof, rattles the windows til they itch to shatter. Wonder why am the only one in this house who is bothered by the noise. Everyone else here is not hearing the din the way it affects me. They don't get headaches, earaches or show any signs of being troubled by the noisy tree.

Stare through the bedroom window. Fog has cleared. Streetlights have been turned on. Turn my head away from the window. Focus on the front door, after hearing a hard knock. It's him, wearing nothing but his black trousers, barefoot, naked from the waist up, hair unkempt, face drenched in mud. Pigs must have been wrestling with him in the pigsty. Next to him, his black mongrel wiggles its long tail, dangles its dirty tongue. Nokati rises from the couch, walks to the front door, holds the latch, turns it right, pulls it and opens the door. He dashes inside the house, breathing heavily, spoiling the house with his bad smelling breath and dirtying the floor with mud drenched trousers and shit soaked shoes. House has become his pigsty. Smell is nausea-inducing and appetite-killing. Phung' Amanzi heads straight for the bathroom, steps inside, closes the door and locks it. My eyes follow him inside. He undresses, gets in the shower, with his black mongrel.

Maya sits on the couch, next to Nokati, in the TV room. They stare at the TV set, say nothing to each other. What can they say? Frustration is eating away at their brains. If I had a tongue I would laugh aloud so hard their eardrums would blast. Would not end there. Would speak out; tell them shit about how they have been mistreating me in their house: leaving me locked in the wardrobe the entire time, not even allowing me to go out at night to play with my friend Sporho. I'll never forgive them for this. Wonder what my friend is doing right now in the graveyard boredom.

Phung' Amanzi comes out the bathroom, a brown towel wrapped around his waist. He joins Maya and Nokati in the TV room. Twins come out of their bedroom and join the family. Silence; the TV is on mute, so is every mouth in the house. Only the wailing of the tree and the sound of hooting cars streaming by and dogs barking after them interrupts the silence at certain moments. Suspect this irritating silence. Gives me so many things to think about. Hope it's not their trick of trying to get inside my head and eavesdrop on my thoughts.

Next to my wardrobe lies the snoring black mongrel. A sticky, red substance drips from the sides of its jaws. I'd like to touch the head of this black mongrel, read its thoughts and watch its dreams. Afraid. Might get wild and bite me. Sporho told me that mongrels, specifically black ones, are dangerous in their sleep because they are able to see you when you are invading their dreams. He had told me that his lost friend, Hlakanyana, a trickster of high note, could watch the dreams of ordinary dogs. He had tried it with a mongrel and the beast woke before he could watch its dream. Bit off his hand, howled and jumped, trying to reach for his scrawny neck. Sporho had showed me the horrifying picture of the injured Hlakanyana, nursing his leaking wound. Still tempted to see what this black mongrel next to me is dreaming about. Yet I fear losing my hand and contracting infections. Sticky substance dripping from its jaws might be a sign of rabies. This month, there has been a sudden eruption of rabies that has infected and driven half the youth in the townships mad and the luckless ones, dead. Saw this on the news.

Phung' Amanzi enters the bedroom am in. He opens the wardrobe next to me, careful not to hit the dog with the door and wake it. He grabs a bottled liquid. Closes the door, walks out the room, out the front door. Lurches towards the zebrawood. Still wailing. Neighbours have been standing behind their fences, staring at our yard, for hours. Phung' Amanzi shakes the bottle, opens it and pours the black liquid on the protruding roots of the tree. Substance sinks into the soil.

Says: Bendigcine iihagu zam Sulila Andifanga.

Closes the bottle. Branches stop waving about, contract and coil into orbs. Noise stops. Neighbours disappear into the backyards of their houses. Phung' Amanzi strides into the house and sits snugly between Nokati and Maya. Now watching a show on the TV with the volume high. A reality show that exposes fake magicians and tricksters.

BLOOD FESTIVAL

Nokati enters the bedroom, a bounce in her gait, her face glowing with intensity. Body robed in her long black dressing gown that hangs and hides her bare feet. Stands in front of the wardrobe, begins to murmur, words hover under her ragged breath. Bangles on her thin wrists make a railing noise – a boring backtrack that aggravates my annoyance. Her eyes are fixed on her gloomy face mirrored in the looking glass, palms glued together, rubbing each other.

Next, her voice rises, shouts out words. Waving her hands, eyes now shut. Long paragraphs, hitting the roof, jumping out the bedroom to echo in the living room. Complicated, I don't catch the words. Words that free me from this wardrobe change each time. Sometimes they come in short sentences. Other times, they run in a series of verses, like this evening's chant.

Have to get out of this drawer, this house, this side of the township. Nail rattles, itching to prick my heart for inventing such thought. As if Nokati hears my thoughts, she shuts her lips, opens the wardrobe, then the drawer. Body loosens. Gain control of my limbs and movements – freed. Jump out the wardrobe. Stand on my feet, so tall my head hits the chandelier. Bobs back and forth. Hold it and make it stop.

Little mirrors decorating the chandelier show me how my hairs have grown so long they stretch to hang on my broad shoulders. Face forlorn, exhibiting a dark aura – it often unveils when with Sporho, my friend, brother. Wonder if he's thinking of me right now in that graveyard boredom he's stuck in without access to social life. Miss him so much I wish to meet him tonight.

Nokati opens her eyes, scans the room, steps out the house and rushes to Bhogrom's cabin. Spend a great while punching, kicking the air, pacing up and down the bedroom, flexing my muscles, winding my neck til I don't feel it anymore: numb. Keep pacing from wall to wall; have not felt such freedom in a long while.

Walk to the kitchen. Tiled floor is awfully cold under my feet, feels am walking on ice. Stand staring at the Rain Horns made of gold. Grab and take them o' the hanger. Weighty. Tie them around my waist. Walk back to the bedroom, grab my black and white blanket and cover my body. If Nokati and Phung' Amanzi ask why am wrapped in this blanket, will tell them that am feeling frigid. But I doubt they will ask. Has always been Maya who reminds me to wear the black and white blanket. I'd always throw it over my shoulders and be enclosed in warmth. Just hope Nokati has run out of umgubo wonyamalalo. That's going to be great; they won't bother me about the blanket. They know it is cold esibhakabhakeni and it's a long way from here to Bhakubha.

Nokati returns, followed by Bhogrom, Mbulu and oohili – all of them fill up the bedroom. All sit down. Maya and the twins are sitting on the bed. Phung' Amanzi opens the bedroom window. Wind blows in, freshens the house. He squats on the carpet, holds the djembe between his thighs, begins beating it hard with his palms. Shirtless; muscles shine with sweat as he drums. He has not said anything since he arrived. Wonder what is going on in his head, inside the head of Nokati and Maya – are not they afraid of what is going to happen tonight at the festival? They should be very afraid. They are going to lose their daughter and the Rain Horns. Want to crack a lousy laugh like that of my young brother, inqalathi, whose name I have forgotten. Have been trying very hard to remember his name each moment his round face visits.

Narrow my weak eyes and look through the open window. Zebrawood is now housing a group of black birds. As soon as they notice that am looking at them, they flutter their wings, shed feathers and fly into the sky. A sign. Never in my entire life have pigeons been frightened by my appearance. Think they sensed something is going to happen tonight. A lot will happen tonight. That is the reason Phung' Amanzi has not said a word and Nokati and Maya have troubled faces.

Listen to the humming and drumming of Phung' Amanzi. Each bassy thud of his palm on the drum sends shivers down my back and the nail loosens. Inside my head I only hear booms. Drown my thoughts. Unsure of what am thinking about. Nothing is clear. It's as if the fog has returned to cloud my vision for good.

Nokati and Maya are now dancing and chanting.

None of them have noticed that the Rain Horns have been taken down. Can't even notice that am hiding something under this warm blanket that has begun to make me sweat. Sweat ifutha and it smears the blanket, making its inside pale. Blanket is mine; nobody in this house bothers touching it.

Oohili have circled around Maya and Nokati. Bhogrom is standing near the open window, ready to be ridden. I have my misgivings. Don't think Bhogrom is able to carry all of us to Bhakubha. Last time he got tired and fell. It was Nokati who had to use her farts to keep us afloat and carry us through to Bhakubha. It was just the two of us. Bhogrom could not handle our weight. Now, it is me, Maya, oohili, Mbulu, Nokati and Phung' Amanzi. Bhogrom's back is not strong enough to carry us all. Oohili should not come along. Too many of them.

Phung' Amanzi stops drum-beating and hymn-humming.

Says, We must go now!

His voice is throaty. He stares at Nokati and Maya, til they get uptight and stare back.

They both stop their chanting and dancing, sit on the edges of the bed, legs crossed, looking at the twitching eyelids of Mfenana.

Nokati nods.

Says, We can't ride Bhogrom. Tata, can you turn us into birds?

Phung' Amanzi grabs the drum closer to his bulging crotch.

Says, All of us?

Not all of us. Maya, Me, Mbulu and Sihamba Ngenyanga. You and Bhogrom go together.

Phung' Amanzi pulls out of his pocket a bottle, filled with black powder.

He stands up, beckons us to come closer to him. Nokati, Maya, Mbulu and me step towards his body.

Well, begins Phung' Amanzi, I still have a little bit of umgubo wonyamalalo.

He lifts his left hand and sprinkles the shining powder over our heads. Shouts, eBhakubha ngoku!

Me, Nokati, Mbulu and Maya vanish from the house.

Bhakubha. Drop down from the sky. Land on our feet on the bridge of bodies. Sneeze out specks of powder. Head is dizzy and my eyes see vaguely. Takes a while for me to gain my normal vision. First thing that hits me is that I have to find a way of going to the river and delivering the Rain Horns. But for now I have to pretend all is normal. As soon as it is time for me to attend the feeding session I'll find a way to the river.

Walk straight ahead; pass the pillars made of skulls. Liquor store is closed though amaBhakubha are standing against the building, conversing with one another. Further up the potholed street, a group of dogs and wolves howl to the moon. Moon has descended, a radiant disc over our heads, lighting everybody's faces.

Walk the distance of the bridge of bodies. Still startled that Nokati or Maya or Phung' Amanzi have not seen that the Rain Horns have been taken down, that am

wearing my blanket, and we have not flown. Wonder if the River Spirit is still around there.

Would be great to have the barrier cracked. Go see my brothers in the eastside of the township. Past the plantations and the vegetable fields and the huts and the houses. Get on the footpath that leads up to the hilltop. Walk for several minutes and then arrive at the Hill of

Bhakubha. Place is packed. Witches from all over the country are gathered here, listening to Gqwirha Elimhlophe addressing them. AmaBhakubha are standing on one side, the visiting witches on the other. Nobody notices that we have arrived. Maya and Mbulu and Nokati tell me that they are going to stand in the front row. Am told to stay here or go to the room of iintsipho. Grin. Wait for them to disappear into the thick crowd. Pretend to be enthused by what Gqwirha Elimhlophe is talking about. She says something about being happy that witches and their familiars from all over have made it here and nobody has fallen o' their balloons or baboons.

Steal my way, escape from the crowd. Head for the room of iintsipho, run down the footpath. Opposite the liquor store. At the room. To my amazement, nobody is here, though the door is open. Iibhekile filled with iintsipho. Grab ibhekile and leave the room. If ever I come across izithunzela and they ask me where am headed, I'll point out that am going to feed in a place that is quieter. They know how crowded and boisterous the room of iintsipho gets. Will think to tell them that Nokati and Phung' Amanzi ordered me to go feed alone. Reason for that they have not told me. No one will question me when I say that. They respect Nokati and Phung' Amanzi.

Walk out the room of iintsipho, carrying ibhekile. Turn right. Tread on the footpath that leads down to the river. Sky here is clean of stars. Hope the rain falls down hard. Confusion will abound, nobody will notice me, everyone will be running around to find shelter. They don't like it here when the rain falls during the festival. How are they going to cook their meat and boil their blood? Fire will be quenched by the rain. If only I could use the Rain Horns to conjure heavy rain.

Soft stones, dry mud, branches and leaves crack and break underneath my weight. Hard feet crush all soft things I tread upon. Feel strange, not sure if am happy or sad, just in the middle of the two, maybe confused. Soft wind beats against my face as I pass through these trees and bushes and shrubs.

Enjoy the mild cold that tickles my skin. A spring in my step. Take out the Rain Horns. Hold them in my hand. Heavy, they are, and something happens in the sky. Clouds begin to gather. Must be the Rain Horns. Have no idea how they work, how they are used to bring forth heavy rain. Gqwirha Elimhlophe used to use them to conjure heavy floods and lightning. Certain spells accompany the boiling of the Rain Horns inside imbiza. I've always been told to leave Bhakubha when the last part of the ceremony of rain conjuring was to be finalised. But now am taken aback by the fact I've just experienced. As soon as I took them out, something strange happened to the sky.

Get to the beginning of the river. Walk up on the footpath alongside the rushing river. River is angry, it jumps up and down and rushes east in a wild flood. Ponder its course before I walk. At the bench. Sit down. Put ibhekile next to me. Don't really need it. Could just get rid of it by pouring out iintsipho into the river. Afraid that the River Spirit will condemn me for doing such without saying something. Spirit cannot demand I say something when I have no tongue, can't speak.

Stand for a long time waiting for a spirit to appear from the waters.

Nothing, nobody comes. Debate in my head.

Decide to sink the Rain Horns without saying anything.

Stand up and walk towards the rushing river.

Hold the Rain Horns in the air, the sky rumbles, and lightning stitches the sky, lightens up the earth. River continues to rush, nothing appears, or happens. Throw them in the river. Wait for a minute. River stills, unmoving, damwaterlike, it doesn't move in any direction. Wait and wait. Nothing happens; the water woman does not come out of the river. What have I done wrong? Turn around. Grab ibhekile, go back to the water, pour the thing in the river and throw ibhekile away. Lands near a rotting log. Hear something cracking, something breaking, from afar. Blanket is opening. Wait til the noise has been quietened. River has begun rushing again. Ponder its course once again before I walk away.

Tread down the embankment. Slowly. Thinking about the water woman. Wonder, was I imagining that I had seen her? Walk til I get to the beginning of the river. Turn left, eastside. Walk down for a long time. Get to the row of trees that are used as a marker. Everyone knows that nobody can go beyond the trees. Nokati and Phung' Amanzi told me that something horrible would happen if I ever tried to go beyond the trees. They never said what exactly. Stop before the trees.

Step towards them. Touch the trees, nothing happens. Decide that the blanket has been broken. Was it ever closed? Believe the water woman. She said that she will break the blanket for me. That means it had been closed til I sunk the Rain Horns. Go beyond the trees and march down for some time and nothing happens to me or anything around me. Take the footpath that leads to ibhuma. Want to see if it still exists. Remember where it is situated even if it has been burned to the ground. I had marked it with the barren avocado tree opposite it.

Pace up. Now am rushing, an excitement has stricken my every step. After hurrying for too long, from a distance, eyes fixed on the avocado tree. Still bare. Get closer to it to observe it. Nothing about it has changed. Turn my head around. Plot where ibhuma had been built is in ruins. Ashes, halfburnt wooden pillars and broken tree branches are scattered about. Patches of halfburnt sail stick out from the soil. They really burnt ibhuma to the ground. Feel needles stinging my heart and skin pores just by looking at the ruins of my first house. Turn my back to ibhuma, walk away and don't look back.

Suspect it is midnight. Stand on the mound, near ebuhlanti. Khaya Township looks small from where I am. Walk down the pathway; pass the kraal, the cabin of S'fombo. Inside, hear him drunkenly rambling. Believe he's talking to himself or to his girlfriend. Tread further away from the cabin, get on the pathway. Winds down and leads me to the entrance to the township.

Quiet. Enter the street that leads me inside the maze-like streets of the township. Empty. Have not been in Khayamnandi since that day the elders took me away from home and brought me to Kwafindoda. Heart beats hard, same rhythm my feet produce as they thump on the concrete street strewn with halfburnt tires, hot ashes, combusted firecrackers residues, and huge rocks that block the way. Pass the rows of churches on Busakwe. Turn left and walk on Botoman. All the taverns are dead.

What a surprise! Last time I was here they were always blasting bassy music! My parents' house is situated down the street, at the corner. Street is empty and quiet. Lights are o' in all the houses. Dogs are barking, others are howling, at what, they don't see me. Have made myself invisible to these annoying beasts.

House of Father and Mother. Lights are on in the kitchen. Enter the yard; cold feet scrape through the branches of the breadfruit tree. Left eye twitches, big toe and the veins on my temples throb. Stand for a moment staring at the fruitless tree and wonder why Mother and Father have grown a tree whose branches are associated with death.

Front door is closed. Walk to the back, the kitchen door – also closed and locked. Cabin I used to live in has been taken down. Only two cabins now. Believe they belong to my two brothers – Mxabanisi and Makhi. Like the ruins of ibhuma, all I see where my cabin had been is all the woods and pillars and iron sheets piled on top of each other. Music softly comes out of one of the two cabins. Not sure which of my two brothers is playing acappella music – is it Mxabanisi or Makhi? Maybe it is Makhi; he's always been the one who liked a!ending church and did not even touch alcohol or drugs or flesh foods.

Go through the wall of the kitchen. Filthy pots and plates are piled up in the sink and a group of cockroaches are engrossed in the food scraps. Walk to the next room. Mother and Father are sitting and watching television in the dark. Stand looking at them; they are focused on the TV set. Want to call them out by their names – Nocwaka and Lum. Want to scream that I have returned. Want them to welcome me home.

After some time, Nocwaka stands up. Switches o' the

TV. She looks in my direction. Am cracking a wry grin. A void in her eyes. She pats the shoulder of Lum. Both look at me. Lum stands up. Both speechless. Shock or excitement? Nocwaka comes towards me, picks a stick lying next to the sofa and points it in the air. Tremble, the nail rattles, isinyenye itches.

Nocwaka nears me, now holding the stick readying it to beat me up. Her face is twisted in disgust as her broadened eyes behold me. Hamba, hamba! Huntshu, moy' omdaka, huntshu! Her shout is menacing. She throws the stick at me, misses my body and hits and breaks the light bulb above my head. Smithereens on my hair.

Lum runs into the bedroom, comes back holding imvubu.

Shouts, Foko'! Foko' s'thunzela, foko' s'thunzelandini!

Turn around, run out through the kitchen door with the energy of a terrified living that has seen the dead. Leave behind screams and shouts and cries. Voices are drowned by distance, the murmuring wind, and the thumping of my feet on the pavement. Don't stop running. Run towards Kwafindoda without stopping.

Feel betrayed, hurt, heart is riddled with needles and nails. Nail in my head rattles without stop, increasing the intensity of my pain. Chest heats up, heart emptied out of my ribcage. Body tremors, skin gets goosebumps. A thousand needles prick my skin pores all at the same time. To ward o' the pain, I think of Sporho, our friendship. His image appears in my head. Stop running. Stand tired and confused near the Somali corner shop. Should I turn left, take Bantu Holomisa Street, and go back to Bhakubha? Think of Sporho. Turn right.

ABOUT THE AUTHOR

Unathi Slasha is a writer from Despatch, Khayamnandi. He is the author of the novella Jah Hills and the chapbook Much with the Dead & Mum with the Dying, or: Rigidities of Rationalism, Camaraderie Criticism & Contemporary South African Literature. His work has been published in several South African and international literary journals. His work is an attempt to reimagine and subvert Nguni folklore to write what he coined as The Unlanguaged World. He is currently finishing a novel under the title The Inciders and working on a collection of essays on South African culture and letters.

ALSO BY CLASH BOOKS

TRAGEDY QUEENS: STORIES INSPIRED BY LANA DEL REY & SYLVIA PLATH

Edited by Leza Cantoral

GIRL LIKE A BOMB

Autumn Christian

CENOTE CITY

Monique Quintana

99 POEMS TO CURE WHATEVER'S WRONG WITH YOU OR CREATE THE PROBLEMS YOU NEED

Sam Pink

THIS BOOK IS BROUGHT TO YOU BY MY STUDENT LOANS

Megan J. Kaleita

PAPI DOESN'T LOVE ME NO MORE

Anna Suarez

ARSENAL/SIN DOCUMENTOS

Francesco Levato

THIS IS A HORROR BOOK

Charles Austin Muir

I'M FROM NOWHERE

Lindsay Lerman

Christoph Paul & Mandy De Sandra

GODLESS HEATHENS: CONVERSATIONS WITH ATHEISTS

Edited by Andrew J. Rausch

DARK MOONS RISING IN A STARLESS NIGHT

Mame Bougouma Diene

GODDAMN KILLING MACHINES

David Agranoff

IF YOU DIED TOMORROW I WOULD EAT YOUR CORPSE

Wrath James White

THE ANARCHIST KOSHER COOKBOOK

Maxwell Bauman

HORROR FILM POEMS

Poetry by Christoph Paul & Art by Joel Amat Güell

NIGHTMARES IN ECSTASY

Brendan Vidito

THE VERY INEFFECTIVE HAUNTED HOUSE

Jeff Burk

ZOMBIE PUNKS FUCK OFF

Edited by Sam Richard

THIS BOOK AIN'T NUTTIN TO FUCK WITH: A WU-TANG TRIBUTE ANTHOLOGY

Edited by Christoph Paul

WE PUT THE LIT IN LITERARY

CLASHBOOKS.COM

Printed in the USA
CPSIA information can be obtained
at www.ICGtesting.com
JSHW082346140824
68134JS00020B/1917